CITRON
PRESS

JULIE **ALPINE**

Julie Alpine is twenty-five years old and lives in London. She was born and brought up in Scotland and studied English at St. Andrews University. Her career to date includes a stint as a 'performer' in a haunted house exhibit, two years teaching English in Cyprus, freelance journalism, and a memorable summer working as a waitress in a cocktail bar. This is her first novel.

She is currently pining for a kitten, recovering from the shock of cutting up her credit cards, and considering a move into pole-dancing.

She has yet to invest in a pair of trainers.

CITRON
PRESS

Fresh ideas from

NEW AUTHORS
CO-OPERATIVE

Published by Citron Press
Connors Corp. Ltd., Suite 155, Business Design Centre,
52 Upper Street, Islington Green, London N1 0QH, Great Britain
www.citronpress.co.uk

This Book is a Work of Fiction. Names, Characters, Places and Incidents are either products of the author's imagination or are used fictitiously. Any resemblance to actual events or locales or persons, living or dead, is entirely coincidental.

ISBN 0754400824

Printed and bound in Great Britain by Esparto Digital Ltd., Slack Lane, Derby.

A copy of this book is held at the British Library.

■ **SENSIBLE** SHOES

JULIE **ALPINE** ■

For my parents, George and Margaret,
who aren't *really* like Kelly's.

ACKNOWLEDGEMENTS

With many thanks to Katherine Hunter, Joyce Morrison, my brother Johnny, my sister Jemma, Nikos Marangos, Hugh Kirton, Louie Skinner, Mark Howden, Jen Millar, Toto Stewart, Sally Laverick, Sue Ellison, Andrea Granat, Donald Morrison, Caroline Roberts, Dave Tyrell, Karen Yu, Susannah Southgate and everyone at Citron, all the ladies behind the make-up counters in Debenhams, and Curtis the porter.

CHAPTER ONE

I am a broken woman. My mother has taken an ice hammer to my self-esteem and has steadily cracked away over a period of forty-eight hours on the subject of where and why my life went so horribly wrong. It was, she has concluded, at the age of seventeen, when I decided to leave school to discover the world, and has subsequently deteriorated with every decision I have made since. I've been forced to flee the family home to which I had optimistically floated for a weekend of home-cooked sustenance and unwavering parental support. (Easyjet had a special offer.) Actually, the main reason for the trip was to escape the shame of not having received even *one* Valentine's Day card last week. I've never been a very good liar. Better to get out of London until everyone stops talking about it and all the nauseating chocolate hearts have been taken off the shop shelves.

So what if I, Kelly Heather Stewart, am twenty-four, going on twenty-five (and thirty no longer so distant on the horizon) without a job to call my own? No property in my name with a nice, steady monthly mortgage payment to make. No car to take me on jaunts to the supermarket with a roomy boot to transport twelve packs of diet coke or large potted houseplants. No man to bring me flowers every Friday and (and this is the one that really does get to me) no cat to run and greet me at the door, purring and winding itself around my slender ankles before eating its little crunchy cat food biscuits and falling asleep on my bed. *So what?* Doesn't the woman who gave birth to me see the logic in the careful and sensitive avoidance of bringing attention to these finer points of my current existence?

Bart Simpson and Millhouse are having an argument in my left ear, Sheryl Crow is crying of betrayal into the other and my eyes are glued to a hypnotic, technicoloured game of Tetris on the computer in front of me. I don't know if I can pull through this one. Before I slide into an apathetic and highly despondent state in which I won't even see the point in washing my hair, getting out of bed or God forbid, talking on the phone (crazy, I know, but I've been there before), I feel that I must make one last ditch effort to save my sanity. This will, of course, involve me writing a list. Or maybe numerous lists. Maybe I'll paper my walls with lists. It's just not the same reading the ready-made lists in compact pocket-sized paperbacks proclaiming the route to serenity, perfect happiness, career success or continuing passion in a long-term relationship at the very reasonable price of two pounds ninety-nine. My lists have to be written in ink, on paper. Preferably the larger sized yellow Post-It notes. They must positively ooze with hope. With motivation and aspiration. With the certainty that the light at the end of the tunnel is in sight. Not only in *sight*, but easily within my reach if I just focus on the task at hand, be it a completely healthy, nutritionally sound shopping list or a note about which charitable organisation I wish to become actively involved in this year.

I'm sure I have some candles around here somewhere. Little red and green cranberry and pine scented ones, left over from Christmas. God, my room is such a mess. I waste fifteen minutes looking for them but it's worth it when they turn up at the bottom of the laundry basket. The smell is reassuring. I risk singeing my newly cut fringe when I lean over and breathe in deeply. I have to force myself into a mood of reflection and self-improvement. I don't really want to dwell on the sad occasion of the Visit Home.

In every flat I've ever stayed in I've always aimed for an environment of minimalistic interior design. It never works though. I'm always stuck with the overloaded shelf effect of the late seventies. I must remember to add Feng Shui to my list of New Things I Want to Learn. I'm probably guilty of some fundamental chin and chang mistake. Maybe my whole life would drastically improve if I just moved my wastepaper basket to a different corner of the room. Mind you, I could probably save money on class fees and the hardback coffee table book by popping into Muji tomorrow. The secret lies in the storage containers, and obviously, how you arrange them. For now however, the candles go a long way towards elevating my surroundings into a glowing, December-scented area of creativity.

I'm determined to save myself a prescription of Prozac. Believe me, St. John's Wort may be a naturally uplifting herbal alternative but it produces nothing of the emotionally numbing effect of those little green and white capsules. I'm all set. My pen is poised and the Post-It notes are sitting expectantly in front of me. God! My nails really need doing. I've noticed recently that my subtly understated French manicure takes on this bluish-grey tinge only a few days after I've spent literally hours doing it. I blame the pollution in London. Either that or my raspberry Body Shop bubble bath, which admittedly *is* a deep purplish-blue colour. But the rest of my body doesn't seem to go blue. Unless I'm out on a particularly cold day and forget to wear hat, gloves and scarf, that is. The British weather is frighteningly grim. I don't understand why anyone would choose to leave a sunny, happy country to set up home here. I don't actually understand why more Brits don't emigrate. Surely the bulk of our nation don't share the financial ruin that I constantly find myself in. Maybe it's just London. If you see a man standing on the pavement with a pile of cardboard boxes in Scotland you just assume he's waiting for a lift home from the supermarket. But if you see a man standing on the pavement with a pile of boxes here, you assume it's his home.

I'm not going to put this off any longer. Damn. I meant to buy a new magazine on my way back to the flat tonight, but I forgot. This month's *New Woman* has an article in it about finding love on the

Internet. It looks really interesting. Okay. Lists! I wonder if I'd be justified in calling them musings? Does that word actually exist? I must check it in the dictionary sometime. Shit, I've lost my dictionary. I suppose my English/Greek one would do. Anyway, I'm just going to have to create some vague sense of hope out of the ashes of my self-confidence. Something that actually makes me want to get out of bed tomorrow. I put my *Saturday Night Fever* CD on and immediately feel a bit better. Right. Where was I?

*

Things I have achieved in the last twelve months

Purpose: to remind parents of what to say about me to other parents at parties

Graduated with a BA degree in Journalism and Marketing. (This actually happened eighteen months ago but is important enough to be included on list.)

Learned how to turn on and off a computer and repeatedly considered enrolling on a computer studies night class.

Held a dinner party for fourteen guests. (Getting in outside caterers did help, although all the organisation and final say on the menus was left to me.)

Passed my driving test on only fourth attempt. (It wasn't half as bad once I applied to do it at the test centre at Hemel Hempstead – London streets are just ridiculously busy.)

Opened a Post Office savings account. (Current balance £76.97 – makes me feel so much better about my £786 overdraft in the bank.)

Frequently bought The Big Issue.

Learned to bake the perfect chocolate soufflé. (Useful for emergency PMT chocolate craving.)

Started buying the Guardian every Monday and most Saturdays in active pursuit of real job.

Things I would like to achieve in the next twelve months
Purpose: to give me a solid agenda for success

Meet a charming, wealthy, well-read, sexy man with a great job involving plenty of international travel and whose hobbies include horse-riding and sailing.

In case of failure in finding a man with all above attributes, meet a man even half as gorgeous as the men that my Australian flatmate, Bruce, who's gay, regularly brings home to torment me with.

Stop aimlessly hopping from one country to another, surviving solely on barmaid/waitress wages and find a permanent job – preferably in a hot, Mediterranean country.

Give a kitten a good home. (Oh, to hear it purring in my ear as I fall asleep at night.)

Win a hideously large amount of money. (Or at the very least, a crossword competition.)

Enrol on a computer studies night class.

Things I haven't done, but easily could have done
Purpose: to put my failings into some sort of perspective for parents

Become an intravenous drug user.

Appeared in a fly-on-the-wall documentary for Channel 4.

Gone to prison in a foreign country.

Become a lap dancer to supplement barmaid/waitress wages.

Sold kiss and tell stories to a tabloid newspaper. (Come to think of it, not socialised with any politicians at all.)

Married a Muslim and had him seize our three children two months after our divorce and hide them at his mother's house in his native Iraq.

*

It is so unbelievably satisfying to have indelibly committed such clear, concise lists to paper. I stick all three Post-It notes at varying heights across the computer screen. I don't use it much anyway. It's one of those things that I bought with the idea that it would change my life. Like my roller blades. And my yoghurt making machine. And my £39.99 cellulite refining gel. Anyway, I think I'm going to survive after all. I'm already remembering things I have to buy tomorrow. Washing-up liquid (Bruce stubbornly says that it's my turn to get it and has refused to buy any for the last two weeks), some Muji A4 files in natural cotton, and a stunning lambswool sweater I've seen in Army and Navy, that my mother is sure to approve of.

Sleep comes easily after I've indulged in a small spliff and borrowed Bruce's bed socks to keep me warm. Oh, and finished off last Thursday's chocolate soufflé.

CHAPTER TWO

I'm holding one of those guns that you have to kind of click open to refill with cartridges. You know, like the ones in fairgrounds where you have to shoot out the target? Anyway, I know there's a bad guy around somewhere and I know I won't hesitate to use the gun. Matt Le Blanc is standing further up the mountain, waiting for me, and I'm climbing up towards him in my furry, yeti style boots which went out of fashion in the eighties but are long overdue for a revival. I'm not sure yet if David Schwimmer is with him but I hope that he'll be there, waiting for me. When I get to the top we can all make a run for the helicopter. Suddenly I hear him calling and I know that everything's going to be okay. My heart lights up and I start climbing faster and faster. Making my way up this treacherous mountain.

'Kelly...Kelly!' 'I'm coming David. I'm almost there... Wait for me. This snow is really tricky.' The vision of David holding out his hand to me begins to fade. 'KELLY, for God's sake, WAKE UP. Caitlin's on the bloody phone and she's in a phone box. Are you awake? Are you even *in* there?' Where else and with who else would I be? Of course I'm in here.

There follows a banging on my bedroom door and I'm rudely propelled to full consciousness. I absolutely hate being woken up and I hate it even more when I'm removed from a particularly thrilling dream.

My imagination is so active while I'm asleep. My sleeping hours are, I'm sad to report, hugely more exciting than my waking ones. This could be due to the fact that over the last few weeks, my sleeping hours seem to have hugely outnumbered my waking ones.

Bruce puts his head round my door and even in my semi-comatose state I find myself wondering for the thousandth time how he has the nerve to be so beautiful without any recognisable beauty regime. He constantly defies the women behind the make-up counters in Debenhams. He has one of those jaw lines that seem to be particularly prevalent in Australian men. Chiselled, I think, is the right term. It may be a cliché but in his case it's the only way to describe it. How I wish that God had used the same tools to craft my thighs.

'Morning sweetie. Are you going to get out of that bed of yours and speak to Caitlin? She's got a day off work. She's already called twice this morning but since it was before noon I didn't think I could justify the risk of entering your boudoir at such an ungodly hour.'

I get out of bed but am unable to find my voice yet. I try to preserve the illusion of sleep by feeling my way to the phone in the hall with my eyes closed. When I pick up the receiver I'm greeted by a beeping tone which I presume means that Caitlin ran out of money. I can't work up the energy to feel bad about it and decide that I must drink orange juice in the next thirty seconds or die.

Bruce is sitting at the breakfast bar. I just love that phrase. Let it roll of your tongue...*breakfast bar*. Having one in our kitchen almost compensates for the thick maroon shag pile carpet throughout the entire flat, which is just *so* passé. Natural wooden floorboards are the way of the future and my first property all of my own will definitely have them. Anyway, Bruce is reading the Mirror. It's actually quite admirable the way that he chooses to read such a low-brow paper with such openness and lack of embarrassment. I could never do it, which is why I'm forced to suffer the Times or the Independent when in public. (Except of course for Mondays and Saturdays when it's the Guardian, which is still perfectly acceptable.)

'Have a nice weekend at home?' Bruce enquires, in a chatty, interested, amicable tone of voice. 'Hideous,' I reply, over my Tropicana, in what I imagine to be a kind of God-aren't-parents-terrible sort of way. 'It doesn't look like my father's ever going to help me out of an unexpectedly large phone bill crisis ever again. Or with rent that I didn't even realise was due for another fortnight but then is suddenly looming threateningly over me. Or even with the money for my flight up to Scotland to visit them. I mean, I visit them out of the goodness of my heart and this is the thanks I get.'

Bruce doesn't look up from his cornflakes. 'Well you're feeling sorry for yourself today, sweet pea. You should come with me to the gym this afternoon and sweat out all that self-pity.'

Thankfully the phone rings at that moment and I'm saved from trying to come up with a plausible excuse to Bruce's preposterous suggestion involving me and sweating. Better yet, a visit to the gym is completely out of the question because Caitlin is telling me to get my arse to Covent Garden for coffee, chat and therapy shopping in half an hour. Caitlin broke up with her completely unsuitable boyfriend, Tony, two weeks ago. Although she's so totally over him, any justification for shopping is okay with me. I suddenly see a vision of one hundred percent natural cotton Muji storage boxes and remember that there is a point to my day after all.

I do getting dressed and make-up in record time and tell Bruce to have fun being strenuous at the gym, and to keep his eyes open for good-looking single men for me. I always ask him that although I'm sure he's usually too busy keeping his eyes open for good-looking single men for himself.

'Remember to bring washing-up liquid home with you,' he calls as I'm halfway through the door. 'I just used the last Tupperware container as a cereal bowl.'

*

Caitlin is standing outside French Connection and my eyes are instantly drawn to the shopping bags she's already laden with. Not just *any* shopping bags, but ones with all the right names on them which elicit a Pavlovian response in me to grab the nearest credit card. We throw our arms around each other, although it's only been four and a half days since we last met.'

I can't help myself. The first words out of my mouth are 'What've you bought?' 'Oh, some amazing things,' she replies confidently before suggesting that we have a drink in our usual café round the corner. Reluctant to delay the shopping – I've got a lot of catching up to do – I agree, on the grounds that a caramel latte is bound to give me added energy for traipsing round the shops.

Caitlin and I have been best friends since we were eleven. Our friendship was sealed over a Torville and Dean skating routine we created on roller-boots in the school playground. I was Dean, she was Torville. I seem to remember that one or both of us giggled so much that day, we ended up peeing our pants. We've had our ups and downs but we still know each other better than anybody else. God, I'm glad that nobody knows me as well as Caitlin does. She's the only person who has ever witnessed me eating Pringles dipped in coleslaw followed by six Kinder Surprise eggs, during a broken-hearted frenzy. I'd been in London for six months aimlessly trying to decide what to do with my life, before Caitlin moved down. The wine import/export company she works for opened its City office last September. She's far more business-minded than I am but she still knows how to have a good time and she'll never forget the art of impulse shopping.

After we've lovingly fondled the items in Caitlin's shopping bags we spend the next twenty minutes discussing the merits of fringes as opposed to long layers clipped back in a middle parting. Caitlin says all the right things about the fringe that Pierre did for me before my trip to Scotland. She even comments that it does great things for my eyes, which are today heavily surrounded by black liquid eyeliner and green shimmery shadow.

She envies me my bravery with colours. So what if my mother tells me that the natural look is far more desirable and that my pencilled on eyebrows are bound to scare men off? Caitlin can be so great.

But Caitlin can also be an interfering bitch. Now she's telling me how she's passed on a copy of my CV to her friend Cordelia (*Cordelia?*) who works at a recruitment agency just off Oxford Street called Big Jobs (or something like that). She's telling me how I'm not doing myself justice by working for a couple of weeks at one bar and then moving on to somewhere new but equally prospect-less. She tells me to expect a call from the agency because Cordelia feels certain that there'll be some reception temping that I'd be perfect for. Don't get me wrong, I know Caitlin means well, and on occasion I absolutely adore wearing smart little suits with matching bag and shoes, but I have enormous doubts about my capability to function in an office environment. It just sounds so creatively unstimulating. 'Well, I hope she doesn't decide to phone before ten in the morning, like certain *other* people I know.' I don't much like the petulance that creeps into my voice. Caitlin doesn't rise to the bait.

During the rest of the expedition I do my best to hide my displeasure from Caitlin, but end up spending £98 in Muji as a means of venting my frustrations. Oh, and I also buy the cute lambswool sweater in all three colours it comes in (slate grey, fuchsia pink and camel). This necessitates the opening of yet another store account. It turns into quite a bargain because, as a new store card holder, I'm entitled to ten percent off my first purchase.

We end up at Oxford Circus tube station where we have to go our separate ways. Caitlin reminds me to expect a call from good old Cordelia. Can't wait. Before Caitlin goes she says, 'Tell me if she doesn't get in touch. I'll mention it to her next time I see her.' Shit, it's not like I'm counting on it or anything. I'm still not *quite* at my overdraft limit.

I virtuously remember Bruce and the washing-up liquid as I pass the corner shop near our flat. Unfortunately they're out of stock. In fact, they seem to be out of stock of a lot of things, although the supplies of dog food and toilet paper are looking quite healthy. I unearth a couple of packets of paper plates and plastic cutlery at the back of the shop and feel pleased that I can be so enterprising in a domestic emergency. I also remember to pick up a copy of the Guardian. I arrive home excited at the prospect of filling and arranging all my lovely new boxes.

CHAPTER THREE

I'm out of bed earlier than usual on Tuesday, probably due to the fact that I was in bed before half past nine last night. I couldn't face being around to watch Bruce getting all dressed up and heading out for a night on the town. I have a wardrobe of great clothes and nowhere to wear them. Or more to the point, nobody to wear them for. The Muji storage system looks pretty good but the effect is marred somewhat by the numerous hardened puddles of red and green candle wax liberally dotted across the carpet. I've learned from experience that it's easier to move house than to extract wax from the carpet.

I'm feeling pretty productive and fly through all the offerings in the media section from yesterday's Guardian. A few distinct possibilities catch my eye. God, there are Post-It notes all over the computer screen. I pull them off and throw them in the bin. I type out covering letters (torturously slowly) to go with my CV, applying for the position of Marketing Assistant at the Battersea Dogs' Home, and another for a Celebrity Co-ordinator for an abused children's charity. I feel that I can relate to children who feel unwanted and unloved plus I like the idea of meeting various celebrities. French and Saunders would be a good suggestion to cheer everyone up at functions. Finally, I write an application to be a reporter with a Middle East broadcasting corporation. I had to stretch facts a little on my letter for that one, but it certainly looks like the most exciting and glamorous of the lot, and would definitely involve working in a hot climate. I'm sure I could pick up Arabic and Hebrew fairly quickly if I put my mind to it.

I'm waiting for my fifth piece of toast to pop out of the toaster when the phone rings and I have the dilemma of either answering it or saving the toast, and eating it while it's still hot. I'm not quite so hungry any more, and go for the phone.

It turns out to be Cordelia and if I'd known that in advance I would have gone for the toast option. I force myself to speak civily but without humility. There's no way I'm going to beg any Cordelia for any damn office job, thank you very much.

She doesn't actually offer me a job though. Instead she asks what time it would be convenient for me to pop into the agency. Thinking quickly I say three o'clock so I'll be able to watch *Jerry Springer* and *Home and Away* before I go. I might even wash my hair.

*

There's this process in recruitment agencies of which, until today, I was blissfully unaware. It involves getting your photograph taken by a chirpy receptionist brandishing a Polaroid camera (damn – I knew I should have washed my hair) followed by filling in forms which simply repeat everything already stated on your CV and then taking a quick 'no pressure' typing test. The grand finale is a personal interview with one of the consultants, who in my case, is of course Cordelia. I'm very impressed with my test results – forty words a minute. That's good, isn't it?

There is obviously some sort of dress code that recruitment agency consultants have to follow. Firstly, they all have to have mousy blonde hair in a mussed up Meg Ryan cut. Twin sets are the favoured fashion choice of the day, and these are complimented in most cases by a chiffony scarf thing tied jauntily around the neck. They all manage to look extremely smug about having secure jobs but simultaneously convey an air of sympathy which inevitably comes across as disgustingly patronising. The most frightening aspect of all this, however, is that a small voice in the back of my head is saying, 'I want to be one of them. I want a chiffon scarf and I want to listen to Heart FM on the radio all day and be constantly reassured that all the clients want what I have. I want to belong.'

Cordelia is brisk and efficient and after a quick chat about my career experience to date ('*Well darling, you obviously like new challenges. Are you sure you're ready to take on the responsibility of a job in London?*') she hands me a glossy 'Information Pack for New Temporary Employees' and explains the importance of time sheets. ('*We can't pay you unless we receive one of these by one p.m. the Monday after the assignment. Is that quite clear?*') After a quick exchange with one of her clone-like colleagues she tells me the alarming news that there's a job for me tomorrow at Cartel Advertising Agency and fills me in on the details. Seems the permanent receptionist is off getting root canal work done. Eight thirty a.m. until six p.m. One hour for lunch. Reception and switchboard. Don't forget that you're an ambassador for the agency and your performance reflects on us kind of thing.

Everything's suddenly happening very quickly here, and I panic embarrassingly and ask Cordelia rather desperately to go over everything again. Three times. Then I'm standing up and walking out and peeking over the receptionist's shoulder to see how my photo turned out. (Surprisingly good in fact. I might ask for a copy.)

*

With a full day's work ahead of me I feel that I have to enjoy my last few hours of freedom. I nip into Warehouse and buy a cardigan for work, which unfortunately, cancels out the amount I'll earn if I survive the whole day tomorrow. But heck! This could be the start of something fulfilling and rewarding. They even offer awards for Temp of the Month and that could be a real challenge. Just wait 'til I tell my parents that I'm going to work in an advertising agency. This one day of work could be the start of the rest of my career.

Next I call Bruce and ask him if he can meet me in a bar – any bar – to celebrate the fact that I've got a job. Bruce is such an easy-going guy. He sets the video to catch *Brookside* and says that he'll come straight from the gym and meet me at six in one of our favourite Soho bars, Freedom.

I contemplate buying a briefcase when I spot a leather goods shop on my walk to the bar. I do want to look the part tomorrow. But on closer inspection the shop turns out to only sell leather goods of the whips and studded body suit variety. I don't have much use for that kind of thing in my life right now. Anyway, I think a briefcase is a bit too conformist for me. I'll be fine with the bigger of my two black Calvin Klein handbags.

I remember my job applications from this morning and stick them in the next post box I see. Looks like I'm sorted for work for the time being, but I suppose it doesn't hurt to keep my options open.

There aren't many people in Freedom at this quiet end-of-the-afternoon hour. I recognise a few from when I worked here and feel a rush of relief that I'm finally moving up in the world. An advertising agency, no less.

I order a double vodka and lime with lots of ice and start working my way through a new pack of cigarettes.

By the time Bruce arrives I've got three empty glasses sitting in front of me and an ashtray somehow overflowing with butts. Bruce has a bottle of Miller and I try to remember everything I had to tell him. I eventually get it all out and Bruce, supportive as always, gives me a crushing hug. He then spoils it a bit by saying that he temped for about eight months when he first came to London before he landed his dream job doing something with computers. His job amazingly allows him to work from home most of the time and still earn big money. I can't understand why he voluntarily gets up so early. Anyway, here I was thinking I was entering uncharted waters and then I find out my very own flatmate sailed the same seas for eight whole months before finding a permanent job.

My head begins to throb and Bruce says we should get back. He doesn't say it in as many words, but I know we're both a bit worried about my coping with getting up at such an early hour.

*

I manage to lay out a pair of black trousers with my new black cardigan and a lilac stretch top before falling into bed. Bruce kindly sets his alarm clock for me. It's a novelty miniature plastic mosque that he picked up on a trip to Abu Dhabi. It can be set to chant alarmingly loudly at seven separate prayer times. Bruce fell in love with its kitsch-ness, and it's not hard to see why. It even has little red flashing lights and stickers of Arabic places of natural beauty. Nobody could possibly sleep through the racket this thing makes. He puts it on my bedside table between my five empty coffee mugs and my collection of blue crystals which are supposed to exude powerful messages of joy and hope. I think they *do* actually work sometimes.

Thoughts are crowding around my head and postponing sleep. I haven't phoned Caitlin and it was her that got me into this in the first place. Will I take the tube and brave the rush hour in the morning, or cop out and take a taxi? Will I be able to *get* a taxi? I'm not usually very good at finding one when I need one, but like chocolates when I'm on a diet, there always seem to be hundreds around when I don't want one.

Maybe I should put on my calming ocean sounds or rainforest birdsong CD. I vaguely hear Bruce talking on the phone. I wish I didn't have to go to work tomorrow. I hear Bruce getting something out of the fridge. I think I'm a bit hungry. I somehow forgot to eat since the toast. I wish I didn't have to get up early tomorrow. I hear the TV going on. I might go and see if there's anything good to watch. Maybe it'll be easier to just stay up all night than try and get up so early. I wish I wasn't so nervous.

Bruce and I watch a film on Channel 5 called ‘He Kissed Them and Killed Them’. It’s as bad as the title suggests but is redeemed somewhat by its mildly amusing sex scenes. The leading actor has some kinky outfits just like the ones I saw in the Soho leather shop. I mention this to Bruce and he goes into unnecessarily vivid details of a guy he once knew who had this whole dungeon set up in his basement.

I head back to my room when Bruce goes to bed. It’s no fun being an insomniac on your own. God! That lilac top doesn’t really go with those trousers. I change it for another which is a slightly darker shade of lilac. The last thought I have before sleep claims me is that I still haven’t done my nails.

CHAPTER FOUR

I make it out of bed at the required hour. I'm so keyed up that I'm awake before the mosque even starts its call to prayer. I brave the public transport system to Cartel's offices in Fulham Broadway and sincerely hope that I don't look as pale and disillusioned as most of my fellow tube travellers. At least the lilac top adds a splash of colour.

I find the office with six minutes to spare and use this time to smoke two fags very fast. I get a bit of a head rush which is not exactly unpleasant. On my third attempt I get out of the lift on the correct floor. Not many people are about yet but a smiling Irish account manager sits me down at the reception desk and goes over what I'm expected to do. (I'm pleased to notice an abundance of yellow Post-Its, although they're only the small size ones.) I listen attentively to everything this Martin guy's telling me, but I think he's going over the top a bit. Surely he's telling me what goes on in an average *week* rather than a day. The meeting and greeting stuff at least sounds easy.

It must be about nine thirty-four when I realise that none of it's easy and I'm feeling so flustered that I don't even have time to keep checking my watch and counting how many minutes 'til lunch.

What have I done to deserve this? I've been entrusted to switching on the security system and changing the video, turning on the TV and computer, answering the phone (which flashes red lights continually), operating the door release button for visitors, ordering couriers to collect and deliver boring-looking brown envelopes which are always marked *Urgent*, ordering airport cabs for staff who have somehow wangled 'business trips' to Amsterdam, calling certain people to let them know when the sandwich man's arrived, distributing the newspapers (not a tabloid in sight), and am somehow expected on top of all this to meet and greet the bloody clients. God, I was naive when I put my nail file and strengthening calcium topcoat into my bag this morning.

I really have to fight back the tears when some fat woman in a horrible lime green suit asks me to make four coffees for her clients. It's so demeaning and I'm terrified to leave the reception desk for even a few minutes in fear of the chaos awaiting me on my return. As I walk through to the kitchen I notice a Richard E. Grant lookalike running around his desk desperately shouting 'Fuck. Fuck. *Fuck!*' I'm careful not to meet his eye in case there's anything that I might be able to do to help.

At eleven fifty-eight my mobile phone rings from my handbag under the desk. Damn. I should have turned it off. The switchboard is already flashing the *calls waiting* warning. Damn, damn, damn. It's my mother. I never actually got around to calling her last night.

She launches straight in. 'Kelly, a letter came for you today from the university alumni society. It's probably another career progress questionnaire. Now I know you don't have much in the way of good news to tell them, but do you want me to forward it anyway or shall I bring it down to London when your father and I come next weekend? Remember I told you when you were up that we've managed to get tickets for *Whistle Down The Wind*? And in the dress circle too!'

I've died and gone to Hell. An exotic Spanish-looking woman in tight brown leather trousers is standing in front of me waving an urgent (surprise, surprise) brown envelope under my nose and the switchboard looks like it's going to explode. I tell my mother in a stage whisper that I'm at work and I'll phone her tonight. Before I press the *End* button on the phone I hear my mother saying, 'I didn't know public houses were open at this time. Everything's different in London I suppose.' I have no recollection of her telling me about any impeding visit to London but I really don't have the time to worry about it now.

I deal with the beautiful woman's envelope and work my way through the calls waiting. Surprisingly I haven't run away by the time a heavily pregnant woman, who introduces herself as Mags, appears to tell me that she's come to relieve me for my lunch break, and asks if I've been managing alright. I smile (probably a bit maniacally) and tell her that yes, everything's absolutely fine before grabbing my handbag and trying not to break into a run for the lift.

*

There's handily a branch of one of my favourite cafés, Ruby in the Dust, directly opposite the office. My eyes hurt with the glare of real daylight as I cross the road. My legs feel weak and it is with great relief that I find a table, light a cigarette (with trembling fingers) and lose myself in this month's *Cosmopolitan* which I'd stuck in my bag with the intention of reading it at my desk as soon as I'd finished my nails.

I devour an enormous Mexican Dish of the Day and feel my pulse rate slowing. (I really must visit Mexico some day.) It's better if I don't think about the four hours that still lie ahead, so I concentrate on a feature in the magazine on Sexually Transmitted Diseases, 'Silent Killers'. After only three more cigarettes it's time to get back to the office. How do people do this every day? I'd rather be a PE teacher than deal with the pressure of a thousand inconsequential tasks heaped upon me on a daily basis, and *that's* saying something.

*

Six o'clock rolls around and a few people have the decency to thank me for my help and say that they hope they'll see me again. Cordelia phoned about an hour ago, probably just to check that I was still here. I wish I'd never even heard her stupid name in the first place. I remember to ask the ever-helpful Martin to sign my time sheet and I stick it in with the rest of the office post.

It's definitely a taxi for the journey home. I just don't have the energy to deal with the tube. I try not to worry about the fact that I was completely unable to enter all the data of the couriers I ordered onto the Excel package on the computer, like I was told to do. Instead, I left all the relevant information on thirteen Post-It notes stuck across the monitor. I'm sure the person who makes being a receptionist her whole life will deal with it efficiently tomorrow. She probably cherished the trip to the dentist for getting her out of that madhouse for the day.

The traffic is so heavy and I only just have enough for the taxi fare home. I give the driver a handful of coins and jump out before he can get grouchy about not getting a tip.

*

In the flat Bruce is talking on the phone to Doug, another Aussie, who works in a dog-grooming parlour in Clapham. His ambition is to work in Vidal Sassoon, but he's forced to clip poodles all day until he completes his correspondence course in hairdressing. How do you do a correspondence course in hairdressing? Practise on your friends, or trudge round car boot sales looking for unwanted Girls' World heads?

I speak to my mother as soon as Bruce is off and spend ten minutes complaining about the day I've had (and it's *my* phone bill). My mother chooses to hear only what she wants to hear, and urges me to keep phoning the agency to let them know I'm available and willing. She also fills me in on the details of the *Weekend Saver* break at the Bloomsbury Trusthouse Forte Hotel that she saw advertised in the

Daily Express. My parents will be here a week on Friday and are keen to come and 'see my little home' and meet the 'famous flatmate from Down Under'.

This finishes me off and I slump on the sofa with a glass of cream sherry, a gift from an elderly aunt, and the only alcohol I could find in the flat. Bruce whips up a couple of mushroom omelettes and doesn't even complain about the tendency of the paper plates to go soggy in seconds. He overheard me on the phone and obviously realises what a strain the day has been.

We discuss the fact that I feel obliged to cook a meal for my parents when they're in London, and decide that the Friday night they arrive will be better than the Saturday. My father refuses to watch *Blind Date*, and Bruce and I don't miss it if we can help it. The video just hasn't been the same since my friend Sarah kicked a glass of vodka and cranberry juice over it while we were choreographing a dance routine to 'Walking On Sunshine' by Katrina and The Waves sometime last month.

I grudgingly phone Caitlin because I really can't be bothered recounting the whole horrible day again, but I force myself. She says all kinds of reassuring things and claims that it only seemed so bad because it was my first day. 'But that's the crappy thing about temping,' I whine. 'It's always going to be going somewhere new and not knowing anyone and feeling utterly pathetic.'

'There's good points to it though,' she perseveres. 'You never have to get fed up of the same old routine and the same old office politics and maybe you'll find somewhere you *do* like and have the chance of a permanent job there. I wouldn't mind doing it myself sometimes. Especially when I'm listening to Edith commenting on the exorbitant price of tights these days for the millionth time.'

Caitlin gets full credit for making things not appear quite so bleak after all. Still, I'm glad that I've got a day off tomorrow. We decide to go to Iceni on White Horse Street on Saturday after getting ready round at her place and watching *Blind Date*. I haven't been to a club for ages.

I'm in bed before ten for the second time this week. It must be because I'm getting old. I can definitely see wrinkles around my eyes if I look in the magnifying mirror. For this reason I tend to avoid that mirror, and occasionally resort to putting on my make-up by candlelight. It's really very flattering, and fine if I'm not going anywhere with bright lights.

I'm lulled to sleep by an old Tracy Chapman album which I recently rediscovered and remembered how much I liked. It's an atrocity that Boyzone were allowed to do that cover version.

*

My dreams are alarming and involve me wearing a lime green suit and appearing on stage with Boyzone. I appear to be at least fifteen years older than any of them, forget all of the words to the song and end up running into the wings in tears.

CHAPTER FIVE

I wake up in the glorious knowledge that I don't have anything to do or anywhere to go. I shuffle through to the lounge with my duvet wrapped around me, lie down on the sofa, and fall asleep again at some point during *This Morning*. Not that my falling asleep is any reflection on the programme. Richard and Judy make a fantastic team and you really get to know the whole *This Morning* family if you watch it regularly. Fred with the weather and his impressive selection of sweaters, and the wonderfully sympathetic Denise. And Raj, with all his degrees and sensible advice. I guess I'm still just suffering from the exhaustion of yesterday.

I decide to go out for brunch and swap the duvet for the camel lambswool sweater teamed with a tight black skirt and my gorgeous knee-high black suede boots with the fur around the top. The Mexican meal yesterday doesn't seem to have done too much damage, but I don't risk checking that with my super-accurate, right down to the very last gramme, digital bathroom scales.

I've just finished putting my hair up when the phone rings. It's Liza from the agency calling on behalf of Cordelia. She asks me if I can do Wednesday and Thursday next week on switchboard at a new radio station in Leicester Square. This is good in so far as it indicates there were no serious complaints about my performance yesterday. Even if I can't use Excel. Lisa talks like we're old friends although we've never met. 'Kelly, sweetheart! I think you'll find this a super place to work. Lots of our temps have really enjoyed it there.' (Well I'll only have the one office to compare it to so I give her the benefit of the doubt.) I'm taken off guard with no pre-prepared excuses, and find myself being all friendly back and saying that of course I can do Wednesday and Thursday. I even thank her about four times before hanging up. At least I don't have to think about it for a few days, and the thought of the money helps me to forget somewhat how much I hated yesterday's experience. And £7.50 an hour is heaps better than I've made in any of the bars I've worked in.

I find five letters for me at the front door. (Two are actually addressed to 'The Occupier', but Bruce won't mind me opening them.) You never know what opportunities you might miss by recklessly throwing away junk mail. See! There's a sale at the optician's down the road and it wouldn't hurt to see if they've got any designer sunglasses. I'm not quite so interested in the life insurance plan though. The next letter is from my grandmother and makes me vow once again to write to her more often. This is followed by a rejection from Sky Television who haven't short-listed me for the position of weather girl due to an 'obvious lack of relevant experience', and another from MTV News who don't want me for the exact same reason. Bastards. It's tough when you're up against cheap labour in the form of fifteen-year-olds who are taking media studies GCSEs and are desperate for some work experience. Oh, and are all a size six into the bargain.

I file the rejection letters into my Rejection Letters File. I religiously keep every single one I get in the vague plan that one day when I'm rich and famous I can publish them in my autobiography and cause unmeasurable regret and embarrassment to a lot of personnel managers.

*

I eat a bagel with cream cheese and strawberry jam (bagels are ninety-eight percent fat-free) in a French place near the tube station and flick through last week's copy of The Stage. Bruce and I both love it, he for the theatrical reviews and showbiz obituaries, and I for the unconventional employment opportunities for resting actors.

I notice a small ad offering £650 for one week's work and decide to call immediately. It doesn't disclose any details but, whatever it entails, that money would wipe off my whole Visa bill. It would be a real thrill to pay the entire amount for once instead of just automatically sending them a cheque for the minimum payment and blindly hoping that the cheque doesn't bounce. I use the payphone at the back of the restaurant because, for some reason, I can't seem to make outgoing calls on my mobile at the moment.

I speak to a man called Tom who tells me his company's running a hot drinks promotion and they need friendly, presentable people to hand out free coffee and tea. He's already started holding interviews, but can fit me in at eleven on Monday. It sounds so promising that I don't even care that I have to get all the way to South Ruislip for the appointment.

I can practically smell the money already, and talk about easy! Old people will regain their faith in the youth of today when I smile and hand them their free cuppa. 'Thanks, lovey,' they'll say, 'you've fairly brightened up my day.' Could even be a chance to meet sexy men when they take a break from their high-powered banking jobs and need a bit of refreshment. The mere prospect of it makes me feel like I've achieved something today, and I don't feel guilty at all when I stop for an unbelievably good back massage from Natasha, at the Top to Toe beauty salon.

*

In the afternoon I take a trip to the Natural History Museum. If I'm completely honest I suppose that I still live in hope of bumping into a

David Schwimmer lookalike. But actually it's all too easy to live in London and ignore the cultural sights that make this city what it is. It's also a good place to escape the cold and the boredom of unemployment. God I hate that word. *Unemployed*. I tend to avoid using it as much as possible. If I'm filling in a form that asks about occupation, I'll usually put freelance writer or archaeologist or anything else which strikes me as interesting at the time. But it is handy getting entry to the museum at the concession rate.

Some of the staff here recognise me because I come quite often. Bill, in particular, is always extremely helpful when I become curious as to how they knew how to put all the dinosaur bits together in the right order. I seem to recall him saying that they just copied the diagrams published by the New York Natural History Museum. I could be wrong though. Bill would actually be quite good looking if he was a few inches taller, although he does suffer from an unfortunate squint in his right eye and has to wear special glasses to compensate.

I can't help smiling as I pass a display case of stuffed monkeys. A sign reads '*Whoops, grimaces and scent marks – these are some of the many forms of primate communication.*' We humans obviously haven't evolved as much as we'd like to believe.

I love the architecture of this place and the little stained-glass flowers on the windows. I also like the clicking noise that my heels make on the marble floors. (The employees all wear sensible shoes which squeak as they walk. The effect is not nearly as pleasing.) A man in a Barbour jacket drags his toddler son past me, desperately saying, 'Come on Gerald, let's go and *learn* something.' A little girl with blonde curls picks up a display telephone to hear the elephants-in-the-wild sounds. 'Hello elephant,' she says, and begins an animated conversation. I predict enormous BT bills for her in about ten years' time. I can relate.

After I've wandered around my favourite exhibits (the diplodocus, the crocodile skeleton displayed with the beads and bangle found in its stomach, the giant moose and the earthquake reconstruction) I spend an hour or so in the gift shop. I buy a Grow Your Own Magic Garden set like the one I had when I was ten. I remember being really amazed by it until our cat stood on it and it had to be thrown away. I cried for hours. I'll give it to Bruce. It will be good for him to grow something other than muscles, and it will brighten up the kitchen a bit. If I remember right, you have to set up the garden, pour water over the chemically treated paper, and watch it blossom in pink and blue over the next few days. It's actually highly toxic.

The weather back outside is wet and windy and even though I didn't bring my umbrella with me, I dawdle past all the travel agents windows to see if they've got anything last minute for under a hundred quid. I couldn't be expected to work in a radio station or entertain my parents if I was enjoying a winter sun break in Barbados. I can just imagine flying off for a fortnight of coconut suntan cream and cocktails. The cheapest deal I can see, however, is £699 and clearly out of my price range. Maybe after the free hot drinks promotion it will be a possibility. Although I will have been forced to endure the Parental Visit and God knows how many hours of being a receptionist before then.

*

I have a quiet Friday night in. Bruce has gone out to some art gallery thing. He did invite me along but I've had enough culture for one day. Being home alone permits me to dine on Choco Leibnitz biscuits washed down with banana milkshake without offending anyone's culinary tastes, and to roll a couple of joints without anyone around to tell me how crap I am at skinning up. A couple of hot rocks drop out and singe the sofa. I spend the next hour or so dreaming about inventing a totally burn-resistant fabric. I would make millions. They could use it to decorate university halls of residence nation-wide and it would also be good for the upholstery in cars. I start writing a letter to my grandmother but keep losing my train of thought and give up. Instead, I scribble a quick list of

People I Owe Letters To on the back of the TV guide. I notice the Steve Martin classic *The Man With Two Brains* is on, and watch it for the umpteenth time amid uncontrollable giggling fits.

Before going to bed I'm suddenly inspired to paint my fingernails and toenails in that really deep, Uma Thurman reddish-black colour. I'm in the mood for a change and it will solve the blue-tinted polish problem. I know that particular shade is very last year, but it's only just grown on me, and I don't really class wearing it this year as a *major* fashion faux pas. I feel a huge weight lift off my shoulders as I survey the finished result and fall asleep with my hands resting palm down on top of the duvet and my feet sticking out the end of the bed in order not to smudge the varnish.

CHAPTER SIX

The weekend turns into Monday and I feel like I've wasted it. At least with a nine to five Monday to Friday job the weekend can be truly appreciated. I've noticed that the people in suits on the tube every Monday morning always have a lot to talk about. The highlight of Saturday was seeing an ugly Sloaney guy called Rupert, whom I met at university, appear on *Blind Date* and not get chosen. It was poetic justice. I've never gotten over him not giving me a part in the Drama Society's production of West Side Story. Going to Iceni was just a waste of make-up. Caitlin and I almost got hypothermia standing in the queue for an hour and a half and then spent most of the night running up and down the stairs in an effort to get warm. I did talk to one cute guy for a while but I have my suspicions he was only about eighteen. Right now I need a man to take care of me. Not one who needs me to help him fill in his UCAS university entrance form. The You magazine was missing from my Mail on Sunday and that's the only bit I ever read.

Now I'm speeding along the Piccadilly line towards South Ruislip and wondering if this is worth £650. I'm sharing a carriage with an acne-scarred solvent abuser (well, he *looks* the type) and six pensioners, two of whom look like they may well be dead. I forgot to bring a book, and so alternate between reading the Dateline advert ('*Your perfect partner might be sitting opposite you even as you read this*') and staring out the window into blackness.

Coincidentally, the solvent abuser and I get off at the same stop. He's two steps behind me all the way to the Hot Drink Headquarters and I'm convinced he's going to mug me until he follows me into the office. It turns out that he's got an eleven fifteen appointment. The bored looking receptionist directs us into a room where we join six other hopefuls. The walls are covered in peeling, pea green wallpaper and a 1986 year planner. I think it might be the storage room. There are a couple of boxes of biros in the corner, and some packets of tea bags. The group consists of a young Sharon and Darren type couple who have probably come all the way from Essex, a man in his forties wearing a Star Trek sweatshirt, a couple of college students, a stunning oriental girl who looks totally out of place, Acne Boy and me.

Everybody is uncomfortably silent. It feels like a waiting room in a family planning clinic. If you know what *that's* like. Except for the heavy aroma of coffee and cigarette smoke which hangs in the air like smog. I sit down at the Formica-topped table and study the forms in front of me. The first one is fairly simple and I fly through it. I insert Cocktail Bar Singer in the box marked *Occupation*. It's the second piece of paper, *Terms of Employment*, which makes me instantly realise that it's been a bloody wasted journey to South Ruislip. I might as well have gone to the Southern Hebrides. The smell of coffee suddenly makes me want to gag. I don't know what to do. Tom's already escorted Sharon and Darren into his office for a personal interview. I think it's me next. How do I get out of here? Everybody else looks pretty calm. Maybe I misread the details. I speed-read the offending piece of paper another five times.

I can't do this. I absolutely cannot do this. Not for a plane ticket to Barbados. Not for an entire new wardrobe. Not for anything. Well, maybe for a regular guest appearance on *Friends*. God, I have to leave. I quietly fold the two pieces of paper in half, drop them into a nearby wastepaper basket, grab my coat off the back of the chair and walk briskly out of the room without looking at anyone. I'm just about to exit the building when I remember that my handbag's still under the chair. Goddamn it. I safely retrieve it and wink conspiratorially at the Star Trek man who shoots me a curious look. I flee before Tom can pop his head round his office door and force hot drinks down my throat.

I get the next train back and try to remember how many people I've told about this interview. My mother, Bruce, Caitlin, Sarah, the postman... I'll have to make up some excuse. I can't say that I didn't get it because it would be unbearably embarrassing to have people believe that I'm not even qualified to hand out free cups of tea. I can't say that I got lost because Bruce went over the route in the London A-Z with me last night until I could recite it in my sleep. But will they understand? Will they understand what it would do to me to travel around Britain for seven days in a *minibus*? Would they see that I couldn't possibly share a motel room with one of those *people* for a week? Jesus Christ! Could they expect me to carry around a rocket pack thing on my back dispensing boiling liquids for twelve hours a day? And wear a fucking ORANGE BOILER SUIT IN PUBLIC?

I get home before one and find Bruce getting ready to go out for a cycle. 'Twenty minutes of breathing in London rush hour air is as bad for you as smoking forty unfiltered cigarettes,' I inform him. 'You should invest in an exercise bike, or even a rowing machine, which we can both use in the privacy of our own home.'

Bruce is too sweet to have forgotten about the Big Interview. I tell him that the drinks company has been declared bankrupt since Friday and that the office is currently being invaded by the bailiffs. He's sympathetic as only he can be, and even does his Every Cloud Has A Silver Lining thing. 'Better to find that out now than to do the work and then have them stick you for the money.' This man is an angel. In fact he's probably the only one who *would* understand my physical inability to put on an orange boiler suit. He has impeccable dress sense. He sets off on his bike ride, undeterred by my health warning. 'It'll come good, Kell. Something will turn up soon. No worries.' I feel really bad about lying to him.

I make a peanut butter sandwich and go back to bed. The only thing that's going to turn up soon is my mobile phone bill.

*

This afternoon I get the best surprise I've had since my younger brother Chris bought me tickets for a Shakin' Stevens concert in 1985. Bruce gets home and tells me to come into the kitchen because he's got a present for me. I presume he's being sarcastic and that he's either going to present me with a free hot drink or a new bottle of Fairy Liquid.

There's a box shaped thing sitting on the kitchen table, with tea towels in place of wrapping paper. Bruce is smiling like it's New Year's Eve. I suddenly get all shy and hesitate to 'unwrap' the gift. I don't even know what it is, but it's obviously not washing-up liquid. Tears start to prick at the back of my eyelids. The only thing Bruce has ever given me before is a kilogram bar of Dairy Milk to console me after a particularly painful break-up.

Before I ruin my mascara, I pull the tea towels off and see what looks like a bird cage. Bruce is saying something about it not really being allowed according to our lease, but that rules are made to be broken and that he couldn't get me a kitten but that he thought I'd like this and that he can take it back if I don't like it and that it won't be too much trouble...

It's not a bird at all. It's a teeny, fuzzy, orange and white hamster with a pink nose and little pink toes. It's a hamster. A pet. For me! I can look after it and it can depend on me and I can tell it all my secrets and problems. I'm scared I'll squash it in my excitement if I pick it up now, so I throw my arms around Bruce instead. It's not only that I love the hamster, but that I'm unbelievably touched that he knew I'd love it and went to all the trouble of getting it.

‘I haven’t made its bed or anything. All the stuff you need is in that bag and I got it a couple of nut sticks and a drinking bottle. And the grain is in the small brown bag. He’s probably stressed from the bike ride. Maybe you should give him some water.’

I burst into laughter at the thought of Bruce balancing a hamster cage on his bike. What an inspired present. I name the hamster Fluffy in memory of my first cat, and spend the next hour or so making his house cosy. He’s even got a wheel.

It’s such a domestic scene when Bruce, Fluffy and I sit down to watch *Eastenders* later. I was so grateful to Bruce that I found time after making Fluffy’s bed to rush out and buy some washing-up liquid. I even tackled the huge backlog of dishes. Bruce was able to eat his spinach pasta off a real plate tonight.

I take Fluffy and his cage through to my room when I go to bed at midnight. Bruce says goodnight to both of us. It’s so nice having company in my bedroom and I fall asleep much faster than usual.

*

At about three a.m. I’m forced to get out of bed and carry Fluffy’s cage through to the kitchen. I can’t believe that something so small can make so much noise. I thought that burglars were trying to get into my bedroom through the window until I realised that it was just Fluffy going round in his wheel. He’s obviously a clever hamster. *And* a quick learner. Still, I can’t sleep through that noise and I’m sure he’ll be happy on the kitchen counter beside the coffee maker.

I must remember to buy a new film for my camera tomorrow and take some photos of him. I fall back to sleep to the muffled sound of the spinning hamster wheel.

CHAPTER SEVEN

The switchboard room at the radio station is stuck on the edge of the building and hazy sunlight is streaming in through the huge windows. The lights on the phones are constantly flashing, but the atmosphere is relaxed. I was so dreading yesterday and spent most of Tuesday convincing myself I had the flu. It was only the arrival of my mobile phone bill which prompted me to report for duty. It hasn't been half as bad as I expected. Either Cartel was exceptionally awful or the radio station is exceptionally cushy. I don't feel too good about leaving Fluffy on his own all day, but I'm hoping that he hasn't noticed my absence. He sleeps even more than I do.

Mick is a reassuring presence on my left. He told me what to do when I arrived, and let me borrow his spare headset. (I did embarrass myself a bit by putting it on back to front, but then I haven't done this before.) He's a solid black guy somewhere in his early forties with a voice as close to Barry White's as I've ever heard in real life. I bet that's how he got the job. The voice is about all they have in common though. Mick has a large collection of euphemisms for the act of urinating. 'I'm just going to splash my trainers,' or 'I must let out some water' being just two examples. Kathryn, who sits on my right, has got used to him. She's petite but compensates for this with her big hairstyles, dangly earrings and huge smile. She's in a wheelchair but I stopped noticing that twenty seconds after meeting her. She's perfected the art of holding extended conversations in thirty-second spurts between taking calls. We answer the phones and just transfer callers through to the right extension. All the names of staff are alphabetically listed in a file beside their relevant extension number. Ninety-nine percent of calls are transferred to the Audience Enquiries Desk. I pity the people who answer the calls at that desk. This job has really opened my eyes to the kind of sad, empty existence that many of the British public seem to lead. Between three and four o'clock this afternoon I spoke to sixteen people who are upset to have missed the address for a free recipe sheet and seven people who are agitated by the poor quality of radio reception they're experiencing in the Shrewsbury area. Yesterday I spoke to someone who genuinely believes that Princess Diana was her sister. Ten minutes ago I had a man who claims to have inside information on a local pub that stores chickens for its bar lunches in a nearby morgue, due to lack of freezer space. Logically, I understand that he's either confused or completely unstable, but make a mental note never to eat there just in case.

During my afternoon break I sit in the canteen and watch people fighting with the coffee machine. Most give up trying to extract the milk drop by drop after five minutes and make do with what looks like a much-needed nicotine fix. A good-looking guy in an Arran sweater comes over to ask for a light and introduces himself as Jake. It's weird not knowing what anyone does around here. It's not like TV where you can at least recognise faces. I haven't actually listened to this radio station very often and I definitely don't recognise Jake's voice. It turns out that he's in charge of all the advertisements. My mind drifts back to that scene in *Peter's Friends* where Hugh Laurie and Imelda Staunton are bouncing around their bedroom creating a jingle for a radio ad. Hugh Laurie's come a long way since then. Amazing really. Imagine that, a guest spot on *Friends*. When I break out of my reverie Jake is talking about how he'd rather work full time with his rock band than hold down an office job, but that this government has made prisoners of all of us. He moves on to a speech about the philosophy of Taoism and starts talking me through his recommended reading list. I just stare at him, surprised by how much he obviously loves the sound of his own voice. I bet he's hopelessly frustrated because he doesn't have his own radio show and has to listen to adverts all day. Imagine how hellish that would be. He doesn't just change the channel like all the rest of us do. It's his job *not* to. I can't work up much sympathy for him though. Why are the good-looking ones always so fatally flawed?

Bruce called me earlier to say that he has to go to Birmingham overnight to install a floppy drive or something. He's not sure how long it will take but assured me he'll be back in time for dinner tomorrow evening. He's innocently looking forward to meeting my parents. I ask him to say hello to Fluffy from me and then get back to hearing all about the flasher who's been exposing himself to Caroline on her way home every evening. By the sounds of it, he doesn't have much to show off about.

When five o'clock arrives and I put on my coat I'm honestly a bit sorry that I won't be back tomorrow. I tell them that I'd be happy to come in whenever they're short-staffed again, and I mean it. It might not be the most intellectually stimulating job in the world, but the last two days have been pretty good.

'Don't think we'll ask *you* back after all the mistakes you've made, Sweet,' Mick jokes. At least I think he's joking. I openly admit that I did make a couple of little mistakes before I'd quite got the hang of things. I somehow managed to put a call for the MD through to the kitchen, and five minutes later I coincidentally managed to put a call for the kitchen through to the MD. I improved drastically after I made a list of all the most commonly requested extension numbers and kept it stuck to my phone. Kathryn signs my timesheet and says that she hopes they'll see me again soon. She wishes me good luck for the meal tomorrow and kindly adds that she's sure I'll find a nice boyfriend soon.

*

I go home via Sainsbury's. Looks like half of London has had the same idea. I grab the last trolley before a harassed-looking woman in a hairnet can get her hands on it. It's always a risk choosing a trolley instead of a basket. I tend to turn into my mother and not park in a checkout queue until the damn thing's overflowing. But then I also hate it when I virtuously opt for a basket and end up staggering to the tills holding it in both arms, my handbag sliding off my shoulder and dangling around my elbow.

I'm making an authentic Italian pasta dish for tomorrow, accompanied by garlic bread. It's a tried and tested favourite taught to me by one of my university flatmates. I think he was from Cornwall. I don't want to risk presenting my mother with anything new and daring. Too much room for disaster. Chocolate soufflé for dessert. I make sure that I don't miss a single thing on my shopping list. I snatched a moment at work to make the list but got distracted and answered a call with a cheery 'Good afternoon, Radio Parmesan'. Knowing that I'm going to have to struggle on and off the tube with shopping bags I restrain from picking up too many impulse buys. I can't resist throwing a couple of pineapples into the trolley though. They're such a hassle to cut and clean but they look great in my hand-carved wooden fruit bowl. Maybe I can use them as the table decoration.

*

When I get home, the flat feels empty without Bruce around. I wake up Fluffy who has somehow managed to sleep through me unloading the shopping and banging around the kitchen just inches from his cage. I give him a piece of carrot which he drags into his little plastic house and starts munching on. Breakfast.

I decide to make the main course for tomorrow so that I won't have so much to do at the last minute. It's pretty easy but the finished product always looks deceptively impressive. Boil pasta. Brown mince in frying pan. Add one can of Campbell's condensed tomato soup to meat. And one of mushroom. Chuck in some chopped onions. Drain pasta. Mix whole lot together. Put into casserole dish. Cover with grated parmesan and bake for thirty minutes. The baking part I'll do tomorrow.

My mother phones and we confirm the arrangements. Her and my father will 'settle in and have a little rest' at the hotel, and get a cab round here at about six. She reminds me that my father is allergic to prawns. I've only known that for twenty-odd years. Perfectly plausible that I might have chosen to start the meal with a zippy little prawn cocktail number. God! 'Something's burning, Mother. I really must dash.' I hang up the phone, count to ten, and run to find my *Little Book of Calm*.

*

I soak in a delicious raspberry bubble bath for an hour. Fluffy's cage is sitting on the edge of the sink. I tell him about my mother. He listens intelligently and looks out between the bars at me sympathetically. I explain how she says that maybe *she's* in the wrong. That she's 'put me on a pedestal' since I was just a kid because of me being her eldest child. And how it's not my fault if I can't live up to her expectations. How does she think that makes me feel? Crappy, that's what. But actually, I don't think it's the not living up to *her* expectations that drives me crazy. It's the not living up to my own.

CHAPTER EIGHT

I open my eyes at about nine thirty and try to remember what day it is. It all comes rushing back to me and I immediately decide to stay in bed for another hour or so. It still feels unnaturally quiet without Bruce around and there's no sound from the hamster wheel. It's not very difficult to turn over and go back to sleep.

The problems start when I wake up again. Somehow, it's three o'clock in the afternoon. I check with two watches and the kitchen clock. And then with the video clock just to be sure. I cannot believe this. My parents will be in London in approximately one hour. They will be on my doorstep approximately two hours after that. Oh God! I'll have to move house before then. I can't let them see the place looking like this. As my mother would say, like a bomb hit it. But if I move, Bruce won't know what's happened. I can leave a message in breadcrumbs on the front path. Shit. Really, I don't think I'm going to have the time to make even a superficial impression on the place. At least not single-handed. I didn't do anything last night, thinking that I'd done pretty well just getting part of dinner ready, and presuming that I'd have heaps of time today.

I have to take some kind of action. I frantically look through my Important Addresses and Pieces of Paper File. I know I have a business card in here somewhere that I was keeping for an emergency such as this one. I think it's bright yellow. It must be here. Thank God! *The Busy Bees Cleaning Agency*. They're local, they're fast, and they have pretty reasonable prices. Well, maybe not exactly *reasonable*, but definitely justifiable in the circumstances. I'd rather hand over all the money I've just earned at the radio station than see my mother's face when she notices the inch of dust on all the surfaces. Or finds Bruce's dirty sports socks stuffed down the back of the sofa. Or stands on hamster droppings on the carpet!

I ring up immediately and the line's busy. On my fifth try the phone is answered by a woman with a heavy Italian accent. (Maybe she can throw in a few cookery tips.) She explains emphatically that there are no Busy Bees representatives available at the moment. I plead for a few minutes and she injects a bit more sympathy into her voice. I bet she's got seven daughters of her own. The best she can do is offer two of her reps from four until six. There's a minimum two-hour booking period. That should be sufficient to make this place presentable, even if it is cutting it a bit fine. Cleaners out the back door, parents in the front door. I opt to pay in advance by credit card in case that farcical possibility becomes a reality. At least I won't have to run around the flat trying to find my purse at a critical moment.

I pick up the top layer of junk from the kitchen and the lounge and deposit it in one big pile in the wardrobe in my bedroom. I wedge the door shut with a chair. I don't know what to do next. I want to phone Caitlin at the office but there's not much point. She won't be able to help. I don't need moral support right now. I need Mr Sheen. I have a bad habit of phoning people during crises when immediate action would be more appropriate. I once called my parents at three in the morning UK time from a Greek island to tell them that I was in the middle of an earthquake. A vase fell over and smashed loudly even as we spoke. What could my poor mother and father do but tell me to climb under a large piece of furniture. When the quake stopped I went back to bed and was asleep within minutes. My parents didn't get back to sleep all night.

When the Busy Bees ladies have arrived and got to work I feel a bit less panicky. When Bruce arrives home ten minutes later I begin to wonder if I haven't overreacted just a bit. Lynn and Marjory don't seem even remotely shocked by the state of the flat. In fact they act as if this is positively tame. I find myself wondering if they've cleaned up after any rock stars. Anyway, Bruce thinks it's hysterical. He jumps into the shower before the Bees move into the bathroom. He tells me about his trip to Birmingham through the door. He's shouting so loudly I imagine the neighbours can hear all about how he put his jeans in the trouser press in his room and watched German porn pay-per-view movies all night.

*

My parents arrive on time and I see my mother waving goodbye to the taxi driver like he's one of her closest friends. My father walks through the door ahead of her. He's brandishing a bottle of red wine. If I've known for this many years that he's allergic to prawns, hasn't he known me long enough to know that I hate red wine? (It gives me migraines and inevitably leads to a bout of cystitis.) But I don't want to appear ungrateful. I'm glad they're both here and I warmly welcome the Terry's Chocolate Orange my mother hands me. I take their coats and put them on my bed in the belief that this gives the impression that I have grown more mature and responsible. Don't ask me why the coats ritual would have that effect. It's a weird reversal thing having my parents as visitors in *my* home for once.

I lead them dutifully through to the lounge to meet Bruce. He's sitting on the sofa reading a magazine. To my eyes, the whole scene looks so incredibly contrived. Like one of those cheesy adverts for certain furniture superstores. He acts like he wasn't aware they were coming. Like this is just some nice, big, warm family surprise. I try not to catch his eye because I feel like I'm on the verge of a nervous giggling fit.

Bruce is perfectly charming. He feigns disappointment that the wine my father gave me isn't Australian. It's the kind of ice-breaking thing that goes down well with parents. Conversation moves along easily and I almost forget that I'm not meant to be enjoying this. I mean, I've been dreading tonight since I knew it was going to happen but it's absolutely fine. I'm beginning to hope we can do this more often. I actually think that the rest of the evening is going to go well. I mean, what can really go wrong? It won't exactly be a major disaster if the soufflé doesn't rise.

*

In the event, the soufflé does rise. Everything else collapses. As we move into the kitchen to eat, my mother makes the most alarming noise, and looks worryingly like she's going to faint. She can't comprehend why there is a 'mouse' in the kitchen. She regards Fluffy's cage as if it were highly contagious. I transfer the offending article to my bedroom and attempt breezily to ignore my mother's hyperventilating. A second large glass of white wine helps. Helps me, that is, not my mother. I have a strong urge to run to the bathroom for a quick cigarette but have to take the Marasetti (I had to make up a name for what I'm feeding them) out of the oven. It goes down well, although I forget about the garlic bread until our plates are almost empty. The soufflé is a masterpiece, even if I do say so myself. I hope that my mother remembers to comment on it to her friend Elizabeth. *Her* daughter makes the 'most succulent lemon meringue pie' my mother has ever tasted.

I'm being lectured on office etiquette. My mother has always been proud of her fifteen years of service for an antiquated Edinburgh accountants firm. Believes they only went into receivership because she left to be a good mother to her babies. Anyway, I'm engrossed in hearing about how important fresh flowers are in the workplace. I completely fail to notice the impeding disaster. My father stands up to get the bottle of wine from the breakfast bar. He's studying something on the shelf above the sink. Before I realise what's happening, he has pulled off a pink branch from the Magic Garden and put it in his mouth. He clutches his throat.

He leans over the sink and starts retching. Everything is happening in slow motion. My mother stops talking mid-sentence (I never do find out why carnations are a better choice than chrysanthemums). Bruce has grabbed the empty Magic Garden box from the drawer and is sensibly reading aloud what to do in case of ingestion.

'Drink approximately one litre of tepid salt water and induce vomiting,' he recites. I hand my father the anecdote and my mother rushes him through to the bathroom. (I try to recall if my birth control pills are in an obvious place or if I remembered to put them in the cupboard.) Bruce turns on the radio in a vain attempt to mask the terrible noises emanating from the bathroom. The kitchen is instantly filled with Celine Dion's 'My Heart Will Go On'. I pace up and down the kitchen a few times and then go to ask if any more saltwater is required. Apparently not. My mother tells me through the bathroom door that my father thought the Garden was made of sugar crystals. Seems that he once saw something like it in a gift shop in the Lake District. Easy mistake to make.

Bruce calls a taxi. I numbly get the coats. My parents emerge and I just know that my mother's never going to remember the success of my soufflé after this little incident. My father gamely tells me that he'll be all right after a little lie-down. I wordlessly hand them their things and kiss them both on the cheek. We all ignore the terrible smell drifting through from the bathroom. In retrospect, Parmesan was not the best idea.

The last thing my mother says to me before she gets into the taxi is that it will be all my fault if my father's not up to going to the matinee at the Aldwych tomorrow. As soon as they're out of sight I burst into tears. Shit. Sugar Crystals? Bruce puts his arm around me and pulls me back inside. Tells me that it's a good thing Fluffy never tasted the Magic Garden. Something about his small body mass and how it would surely have been fatal. I try to stop myself wishing that it had been my mother who ate the bloody tree and decide to leave all the cleaning up for the morning.

CHAPTER NINE

It's been almost a week since the night of my parents' visit but the full horror of it is still fresh in my mind. *Whistle Down The Wind* went a long way towards redeeming my mother's weekend in London but my father is still complaining of a sore throat. I hope that it's just one of those things that we can laugh about in years to come. Maybe by the end of the next millennium. Fluffy's still offended by my mother's low opinion of him. Caitlin's been no fun at all these past few days as she's stuck in bed with the flu. I spent three hours yesterday masochistically escaping into the blue skies and golden beaches of travel brochures. I needed *something* to calm my nerves after I narrowly missed being smothered under a pile of clothes, old newspapers and empty diet coke cans when I made the mistake of opening my wardrobe door. I hadn't needed anything from in it until now.

A rejection letter arrived today from that charity I applied to. Seems the position has been filled by someone who's been doing the same thing at another charity for the last fifteen years. Lucky for them I hadn't contacted French and Saunder's agent yet. I applied for another six jobs on Monday, the best of which would involve researching travel brochures for an over fifties holiday company. Twelve weeks of travel a year. I'm now taking a break from applying for jobs. It's about time I was headhunted.

And I seem to be spending more money on stamps and Please Do Not Bend envelopes than on anything else. I mean, I have a hamster to feed, for God's sake.

I'm on my way to meet my Irish friend, Declan. We met when we shared the same social anthropology tutorial group in first year at university. We've never lost touch, although communication is sporadic. Neither of us travelled any further down the anthropological road. He's just started a new job in Surrey as a town planner. I think he misses the green hills of County Wicklow but took the job to be closer to his girlfriend Jenny.

I walk past a mother and child begging in the underground. They're here every day, the woman crying out mournfully for spare change. I act like I don't even see them. Two minutes later when I'm standing on the platform waiting for my train I feel hideously guilty. This always happens. London can be an inhospitable place.

Declan's already got a coffee in front of him when I arrive at the bistro on Long Acre. 'Hey, girl. You're looking good.' He's come straight from some meeting, and is in a dark grey suit. I can't help noticing that he's looking pretty good himself. If he ever decided to leave Jenny, I'd be happy to run away with him back to his homeland. Or maybe we could emigrate to Australia. Lots of Irish there. I promptly curb this train of thought when he proudly tells me that Jenny's pregnant and that they're planning a small June wedding. I try and quash the small voice at the back of my head that's telling me It's Starting. Soon, all my friends will be married off and I'll be a sad, lonely old spinster. I don't want to spend what little time we have together complaining about my hard luck of late, but Declan has always been pretty perceptive.

'Look babe, nobody makes you angry or happy. You choose to make yourself angry or happy based on how you accept other people's behaviour. You've got a lot going for you. You just need something to throw all that energy of yours into.' (*Energy? Me?*) 'I've got a friend I think you should meet. Her name's Lucy and as long as you're not working you should see if she could use some help. She couldn't pay much, but she might show you how to stop fighting what you can't change and start feeling good about what you can.'

'What is she?' I ask suspiciously. 'A hooker?'

Turns out Lucy does something involving children with learning disabilities or something. Got a big lottery grant last year. She must be good. From what I've heard, getting a lottery grant is almost as difficult as winning the actual jackpot. Rather appropriately, I jot down the number Declan gives me on the back of an old (needless to say, unsuccessful) lottery ticket.

We lunch on baked potatoes washed down with strong cider. A throwback to our university days. Time flies. It feels good to laugh. One memory follows another and I marvel at the way that everything always seems so much better when you're looking back on it. I spent my student years alternating between eating pizza in front of the telly and agonising over the size of my bum. It's three o'clock already and Declan has to leave. He makes a point of telling me off for smoking too much and I grab his stomach and tease him that he's drinking too much. (His stomach feels surprisingly taut. I've forgotten what men's stomachs feel like. It's been *so* long.) We promise that we'll see each other again soon and go our separate ways. He shouts over his shoulder that I mustn't forget to speak to Lucy. I notice that Declan's carrying a briefcase. We're all growing up.

*

Somehow I've managed to lose my tube ticket. I always keep it in the right hand pocket of my coat or the side section of my bag, or sometimes in the back pocket of my trousers if I'm wearing trousers. It's totally not in any of those places. I feel around for it pointlessly for a while until I notice a hole in the seam of my coat pocket lining. It's a pretty big hole. If Bruce was here he'd tell me to look on the bright side and be glad that my keys weren't in that pocket. But he's not here and I'm hugely pissed off. It's the little things like that which really get to me. The Alanis Morissette syndrome of finding ten thousand old tube tickets in my bag when all I need is today's.

I grudgingly join the slow-moving queue for the ticket booth. It would be too much to hope for to have change for the machine. Shit. Why me? A moment later I feel a tap on my shoulder and I turn round. God has suddenly smiled down upon me. I find myself looking up into the most incredible face. Huge dark eyes fringed by long black lashes. A positively aquiline nose. A wide mouth with generous lips. About two days' worth of stubble. Black tousled hair. The owner of this miracle is smiling at me. 'You dropped this,' he says, in an accent that I don't immediately recognise. I look down and see that he's holding last week's list of Things To Do. It must have fallen out of my bag when I was scrabbling around in search of my ticket. I've never experienced this Mills & Boons reaction to a man before and I wish that I was sitting down. He must be able to read my thoughts. 'Listen, I hope you do not think I am terribly forward. I do not usually do this, believe me.' (The way that he's looking at me, I'd believe anything that came out of his beautiful mouth.) 'This line is too slow and if you do not have anywhere to go in a hurry, would you care to join me for a coffee?' This is fate. Destiny. If I hadn't lost my ticket I would already be halfway home. This kind of thing is unlikely to ever happen to me again. It takes me about half a second to decide to throw caution to the wind. Who wouldn't care to join him for a coffee?

He suggests a quiet bar only about two seconds from the place where I had lunch with Declan. I nod mutely, still wondering if this is some kind of hallucination brought on by the cider. I wonder if anyone who noticed me with Declan is now noticing me with another man. If so, I must look like a complete hussy. I have to admit, I kind of like that idea.

We sit down in an empty corner and he orders two coffees without even asking me. He's so masterful. I've only known him for about eight minutes and I'm already pretty sure that he possesses every single attribute I've ever hoped for in a man. And others that I hadn't even thought about.

He introduces himself as Stelios Dimitrius (he pronounces it Thee-mee-*tree*-oos) and tells me that he comes from a small village in Cyprus, called Kathikas. Kelly Stewart sounds like such a mundane name compared to his. I've always wanted a more interesting name. In primary three I told friends that I was called Kelly Le Coq Sportif. It was the only foreign-sounding thing I knew at the time. I tell him that I worked in a bar in Greece for a while and embarrass myself by mispronouncing the handful of Greek words that I know. It doesn't matter. He doesn't mind! He is attentive and interesting and wants to know all about me.

I inevitably get onto the subject of how I'm looking for a job and that I feel like giving up because it's so difficult to even get a foot in the media company doors. He nods intelligently and murmurs something about it all being in the *who* you know rather than the *what* you know. He completely understands. He makes a steeple of his fingers and rests his chin upon it. I feel like there should be someone behind me taking pictures of him. He tells me that it's so strange us meeting the way we did. He says that it's destiny. Oh my God! He believes in destiny. I'm having difficulty focusing on what he's saying. All I seem to be able to take in is the *way* he's saying it. In a sexy way. In a way that says he's interested in me. I wish I could just press pause for a second and go and phone Caitlin. I'm struggling so badly to appear calm and collected. It gets even harder to be cool when he starts telling me that he might be able to help me. There's a job that he thinks I'd be perfect for. He explains that he runs a video production company called 'Simply the Best'. His partner is an Egyptian called Tomas. Anyway, they produce video guides of luxury hotels and restaurants around Europe and they're looking for someone to present the films. Like being a Blue Peter presenter but a hundred times more glamorous. It really *is* destiny. As soon as he saw me he thought I might be the girl they're looking for. 'Not only professionally I think. You might be the girl *I* am looking for.' I can't deal with the implications of what he's saying at this precise moment. I store his words away in a part of my brain from which I can take them and marvel at them at some later date. When he's not sitting barely two feet away from me. He tells me that he obviously doesn't have the final say over such matters, and that it's vital for Tomas to meet me as well. I tell him, in as normal a voice as I can manage, that I don't see a problem with that. That any day is good with me. That the next month or so is actually pretty quiet. He hands me a business card with black embossed writing. He points to the address: *Suite 3, Shelbourne House, Berwick Square, WC1*. (Even the *address* sounds glamorous.) I give him my phone number and he tells me to turn up at two o'clock next Friday. I do the maths and realise that that's a whole eight days from now. I suppose I look a bit crestfallen because he quickly explains that he's got a hectic schedule over the next week and that he'll be counting the days until he sees me again.

He lifts up my hand and kisses it, letting his lips brush against my skin seductively. He stands up and I sit there paralysed, gazing up at him. 'Until next time, *koukla mou...*' Somehow, over an hour has elapsed since the tube station. I watch him walk to the door, and leave. He doesn't look back. *Stelios Dimitrius.* I roll the words around my head. I tear open a new pack of cigarettes and can't find the energy to move until three diet cokes later. Even then it's a struggle, and it's only the thought of getting to a phone and speaking to Caitlin that propels me out of the chair.

CHAPTER TEN

People born under the sign of Aries are enthusiastic, impulsive, impatient, ambitious and determined to get where they are going by the shortest possible route and in the shortest possible time.

I'm in one of those moods where I religiously read my horoscope and blatantly disregard the bad stuff. I'm even looking forward to my birthday which is in a couple of weeks. Things are going my way at last, and I think I deserve it. It's been too long since anything really exciting has happened to me. Apart from Fluffy, that is. Probably the last time was our family holiday to DisneyWorld in 1991. (Chris and I were eating pancakes with maple syrup for breakfast and Mickey Mouse came and sat down at our table. I've got the photos to prove it.)

I'm back at the radio station on Monday and Tuesday. Yesterday was pretty slow but today is okay. Kathryn is enthralled by the mental picture I've vividly painted of Stelios. Although he's as close to perfect as it's possible to be, the story of our fatalistic meeting is embellished somewhat each time I tell it. I've added a bit about how he had tears in his eyes the first moment he saw me. And that I remind him of his first love who died in a tragic diving accident. Caitlin's convinced that I'm about to elope and spend the rest of my life in an idyllic mountain village, riding donkeys, eating pitta bread with everything and learning to like olives. My mother, however, has warned me to steer clear of 'Latin' men. According to her, any man who lives south of Dumfries is a philandering, gambling, heavy-drinking, heart-breaking, hair-grease-wearing Waste of Time. My switchboard is flashing. I reluctantly break off from the conversation about the latest Bill Clinton sex scandal. It's a nervous sounding woman ringing to enquire about the station's 'Putting Lonely Hearts Together' show. I can't help but feel a little smug. A few days ago that could have been me. I was even seriously considering contacting London Weekend Television to find out where and when the next auditions for *Blind Date* are being held.

Bruce has got a new man in his life too. Seems like more went on during that trip to Birmingham than I heard about at the time. His name is Bill and like Bruce, he does something with computers. I met him last night when he came round to return Bruce's blue Billabong fleece top. I'm a bit miffed. Bruce never lets *me* borrow that top. Bill's almost as tall as Bruce but much skinnier. Nice eyes behind what I'm pretty sure are Armani glasses. Easy smile. Big ears. Frankly, however, I've seen Bruce do better. Anyway, I know that Bruce is hoping that Bill is going to become a permanent fixture in his life. I'm happy for him. He's been a tart for far too long. Bruce, Bill, Caitlin and I are going to Pizza Express for dinner tonight. Maybe one day Bruce and Bill can double date with me and Stelios. But I'm not sure about that yet. I've noticed that Mediterranean men are not very accepting of homosexuality. I get the feeling that Stelios is very open-minded though. It shouldn't be a problem.

Five minutes into my afternoon cigarette break, Gary, a tall, good-looking black guy from the post room, comes and asks if he can sit at my table. I'm thrilled when I realise that there are about five empty tables in here, any of which he could have chosen. That old saying pops into my head, *it never rains but it pours*. I've noticed Gary around before, and have found myself wishing that I'd one day have the chance to ask him how he got the long, faded scar under his left eye. I don't think this is the right moment though – too soon. I like the way he holds his cigarette. Maybe he decided to approach me today because the usual look of desperation in my eyes has disappeared. I'm hugging the thought of Stelios and Friday's upcoming meeting to myself like a wonderful secret. Except that it's not a secret. I even phoned my friend Sally in Greece to tell her about him. (The last time I spoke to her was eight months ago.) Happiness is meant to be shared. I like Gary's voice. He's asking me if I'd like to come for a drink at the pub round the corner after work. (The one which allegedly stores its chickens in the morgue.) There was a time when I would have leapt at the chance and blown off the plans with my friends, but I don't feel the need any more. I tell him that I'm busy and that maybe we can do it some other time. (No point in burning bridges.) He takes it well.

The last couple of hours in the afternoon pass uneventfully, except for Mick spilling a mug of tomato soup over his switchboard. The buttons are still a bit sticky. Kathryn seems to think that there are some extra shifts over the next few weeks and says that she just *has* to hear the next instalment in the Stelios story. I might have only worked here for a few days in total, but I'm getting to feel like I'm one of the team. Next thing I know I'll be wanting a locker with my name on it, like everyone else.

*

I get the tube, sardine style, to Leicester Square. I'm cutting back on getting cabs while my bank balance hovers precariously around the Agreed Upon Overdraft Limit.

Caitlin and Bill have discovered each other outside the restaurant, and are chatting away like they're old buddies. Bruce arrives a few minutes after me and we all head for the warmth and delicious smells inside. I'm feeling a bit weak. I think it's because I've only had one ready-to-drink can of strawberry Slim-Fast all day. Meeting Stelios has filled me with some long-forgotten dieting zeal. I even go as far as ordering a mixed salad for my main course, although I'm not virtuous enough to sacrifice a starter of garlic dough balls.

Bill turns out to be very funny. We're all captivated by his account of the time he won £300 worth of His 'n' Hers lingerie as a runner-up prize in a magazine competition. He was supposed to go and do a photo-shoot for the magazine with his girlfriend. When they heard that he was planning on bringing a six foot four Swedish guy with him, they cancelled the date. Claimed to have camera problems!

The dough balls are so fantastic. Absolutely dripping in butter. When the next course arrives I feel horribly cheated by my stupid, boring salad, and end up eating a quarter of Caitlin's Four Seasons pizza too. If the calories aren't coming from my plate, they don't really count. Caitlin and I discuss the dilemma of what I'll wear on Friday. It has to be something smart, but not too formal. Something sexy, but not too revealing. Some of my clothes still don't fit me since Christmas. I dismiss our first fifteen ideas and end up gratefully agreeing to borrow Caitlin's black cardigan with the indigo appliqué detail and the three-quarter length sleeves. And the slightly see-through matching top to go under it. It'll look good with my blue skirt with the daring slit up the thigh and my black suede boots. I'm not sure about which handbag though. I might have to go out and look for one before then. Never underestimate the importance of accessories. And I've already booked an appointment with Pierre. He's going to put my hair up in this amazing style I saw in *Cosmo*. Caitlin's got her eye on a guy who she met this week. He looks after one of her company's big wine accounts. He's French. I don't need to hear much more. If he's French she should go for it, even if only to see if what they say about French lovers is true. She says she's not so sure though. She's got a feeling that the first time she met him he was wearing a wedding ring, and that it had disappeared by their second meeting. Small details, I assure her. She shouldn't let that put her off. I don't actually think for a moment that she *was* going to let it put her off. She was just looking to me for a second opinion. With good-looking, interesting men it's my belief that you should act first, ask questions later. There are too few chances around to pass up on a good one.

After numerous cups of coffee and cigarettes we make a move. Caitlin's got to go home and prepare for a presentation she's giving tomorrow. Paul, the French guy, is probably going to be there and she wants to impress him. I don't know how she understands Powerpoint. It's one of the things they cover on the computer course that I'm still considering. I just don't know *when* I'll find the time though. Bruce and Bill are continuing the evening in a wine bar round the corner. I'm certainly not going to tag along and be a gooseberry. I've got lots of things to do anyway. Paint my nails (I'm going back to the French manicure look). Watch a Simpsons video that I borrowed from Sarah. Read a magazine. Let Fluffy out for some exercise. Dream about Friday.

*

When I get home I discover that I've run out of *Natural Ivory* nail varnish. I can't find that video. I've already read the magazine. Fluffy's still sleeping. I'm left with only one option. I remember a second cousin who lives in Bristol, and decide to phone her for a friendly chat. It's great phoning people when you have good news to tell them.

After that, I find the Mirror, which Bruce has left in the kitchen. I can't help checking my horoscope.

Be patient. You'd like to get things settled. Wait until Mercury ends its retrograde cycle on Friday (Friday!) *and you'll avoid complications. Also, you'll experience happy developments on the romantic front, or offers involving travel or new career prospects.*' (Both, I hope.) *Watch your health. Avoid high-fat choices today.* (Well, that's an obvious reference to the dough balls and pizza.)

I go to bed happy. Horoscopes are just so great. What insight! I've cut out today's and stuck it in one of my files. I know I'll want to look back on it in fondness one day.

*

I dream I'm on a desert island and the only food is dough balls, platefuls and platefuls of them. Bill is with me. We wade into the bright blue water and start swimming. He's wearing a frilly pink bra and knickers. Suddenly I see a shark heading straight for me. I try to scream. The dream changes. I see my face on the front cover of National Geographic magazine. My mother is standing with her hands on her hips, wearing a pair of wellington boots. She's waving a copy of the magazine under my nose and shouting that I've got too much eye make-up on.

I wake up and toss and turn for a while. I'm pretty sure the weird nightmares are caused by too much cheese at dinner.

CHAPTER ELEVEN

I have spent a thousand nights at home, on my own, bored out of my mind, desperately wishing that something exciting would happen. Maybe Noel Edmunds would phone me, and I could tell him exactly what I think of him, live on national television. Or a breathtakingly good-looking Encyclopaedia Brittanica salesman would ring my doorbell. Or I'd hear a strange mewling sound from outside my window. Discover a litter of abandoned Persian kittens on the front path. Adopt all six. Something along those lines. Tonight however, I am relishing the thought of having a bath, positively steaming with essential oils. Bleaching the faint (but *I* know it's there) shadow of dark hair on my upper lip. Practising being a TV presenter in front of my dressing table mirror. Tonight of course, is the night that something exciting *does* happen. Not *good* exciting, but exciting nevertheless.

The last time I spoke to Caitlin was at one o'clock today. The presentation went better than she'd hoped for, even in her wildest dreams. Paul *was* there. He complimented her on her work. And asked her to dinner on Saturday night. She was ecstatic. Which is why I can't understand it when she phones me in the middle of *Eastenders* in floods of tears. Unintelligible sounds are coming out of her mouth. She *never* usually misses *Eastenders*. It's scary to hear her like this. She's always so together.

It's usually *me* sobbing melodramatically down the phone. I'm not very good at being the one providing the verbal Kleenex. In the end I give up trying to translate the noises she's making, and tell her to jump into a taxi and get herself round to mine as fast as she can.

She arrives here twenty minutes later, and I can fully understand the hysteria. I try not to let myself appear visibly shocked, but I have a bad feeling that I closely resemble a goldfish. It takes me a good thirty seconds to close my mouth properly. Caitlin's once corn-coloured, dead straight shoulder-length hair is now a mousy brown arrangement of tight curls, barely reaching the top of her ears. She reminds me of my primary three teacher, Mrs Ethel Sutherland. I push this thought quickly out of my mind. My first reaction is to give her a hug. This gives me a moment to compose myself and think about what I can possibly say. But I can't actually come up with anything to say. I can only make soothing noises and pour her a mug of red wine. (The bottle from my father.) I'm desperate to know what possessed her to go for such a radical change. (And how much she's planning to sue for.) The sad story unfolds. She was feeling on top of the world after Paul had asked her out. Probably felt pretty invincible. Decided to reward herself with the afternoon off and a trip to the hairdresser's. Wanted some more body in her hair. Some *Oomph!* (And how many of us can honestly say that we haven't been *there*?) She took a picture from a magazine and the hairdresser said that he could achieve the exact same effect by using a gentle body-wave on her hair and by adding some caramel-coloured lowlights. Caitlin emphasised that she did not want to end up with an eighties-style spiral perm. (Never again, we both vowed at fifteen, when our matching perms had grown out halfway and created a particularly horrible effect.) But something went terribly wrong. Maybe the girl entrusted with watching the clock got distracted by some hair on the floor that was crying out to be swept up. Or a phone call from her boyfriend, Jason. Whatever the reason, the results are the same. Catastrophic. Maybe she should take a holiday until it's calmed down a bit. On second thoughts, that won't work. There's no way she'd be able to take six months' holiday leave at such short notice.

There might not be anything I can say to make things better, but I'll be damned if I'm just going to stand back and dumbly survey the damage. I get my sharpest scissors (my nail ones), a packet of semi-permanent hair colour (in *Burnt Copper*) and firmly keep Caitlin away from all mirrors. She's quietened down a bit now. She's just making little hiccupy sounds. The wine is taking effect. She actually drops off to sleep once or twice as I deftly work away at her hair. This is where all those years of getting *Looks* magazine comes in useful. There are a couple of moments when I think that I should stop before I go any further, and attempt to locate a 24-hour mobile hairdresser in the Yellow Pages. I've got a vision though, and stoically persevere.

A mere three hours later, the transformation is complete. I think that I've done extremely well in spite of inferior tools and the odds being against me all the way. I'm still absolutely terrified though when I bring back the bathroom mirror and hold it up in front of Caitlin. She lifts her head up and looks at herself. What she sees is a very short cut, with small, sharp sections pulled forward onto her temples and above her ears. The colour is bold and sassy. The whole look is finished off with hair wax. Caitlin stares into the mirror. I stare at Caitlin. Hours seem to drag by. Finally, I see a tear roll out of her left eye. I start to reach for what's left of the horrible red wine. Now Caitlin is going to hate her hair, *and* me. I'm waiting for her to lose control and start ranting and raving at me, which is why I'm so taken aback when she kisses me on the cheek and says only two words: 'Thank you.' I'm saved, and now that I can relax, I can also see that she *does* look great. Maybe not how she imagined she'd look when she woke up this morning, but great in a 'it'll take a bit of getting used to' kind of way. Her unusual greeny-blue eyes are really complimented by the new hair colour, and I've never appreciated the shape of her jaw line until now that it's not covered by hair.

Caitlin leaves at half past eleven, resolving to wow them at the office in the morning. Suicide is no longer an alternative. I've diverted a disaster but am soon going to have one of my own if I don't start getting organised for tomorrow. Time limitations force me to forgo the bath, but I have a whole long list of other things to do. I'll definitely have to put off cleaning Fluffy's cage until another time. I must spray some air freshener around the kitchen.

*

I've just finished applying the Jolen facial bleach to my upper lip and am preparing to recline on my bed for the required ten minutes when the phone rings. Bruce is out with Bill for the third night in a row. I debate just letting it ring, but I'm not the kind of person who can ignore a ringing phone. Unless I'm asleep, that is. I waddle through to the kitchen, my hand cupped under my mouth in case any of the bleach mixture falls off. (That's the last thing this carpet needs.) I try not to make any sudden head movements, and say hello without opening my mouth too wide.

'Excuse me, but is that Kelly?' says the unmistakable voice of Stelios Dimitrius. 'Uh, yes, it is,' I reply stupidly. 'I hope I did not disturb you from something important,' he says. (He's so considerate.) My hand that's not holding the receiver is still held at the ready under my mouth. Some of the white gunk smudges onto the phone. I do my best to limit my facial movement as I speak.

'No, no, no Stelios!' (Damn. Too many 'no's.) 'I was just reading that new book by...' (God, who's written a cool new book recently?) 'by Jane Austen,' I finish lamely. Either there's a bigger language barrier than I previously thought, or Stelios is just too polite to comment on my enormous literary mistake.

'I just want to make sure that you have not forgotten tomorrow and that it is still convenient for you. I think that you are going to be a natural.'

'I haven't forgotten. It's still fine,' I say uninspiringly. I can't flirt at such short notice or in such physically uncomfortable circumstances. The bleach is starting to fall off in clumps and I have to get to a piece of cotton wool fast.

'I look forward to it then. I have been counting the days like I told you I would. Goodbye for now, my Kelly.'

I am sincerely glad that he's been counting the days. But I should have been counting the minutes. I'm probably going to break out in an allergic rash in the shape of a moustache. My television career will be over before it's ever begun. I say goodbye, in what I imagine to be a sexy purr, but it's too late, the phone is already dead.

I can't move for a minute or two. I just stand here, holding the phone to my ear. The full realisation of how crappy I must have sounded is hitting me. Some more bleach plops off onto the breakfast bar, and I stare at it forlornly. There's a sound from the front door, and Bruce and Bill appear. They're rosy-cheeked from the cold night outside. Or maybe it's just the bloom of young love.

'Hey, Sweetie,' says Bruce. 'What's with the moustache?' I calmly hang up the phone and start to edge my way towards the door. 'Who the hell are you speaking to at midnight anyway? Is everything okay?'

'Everything is abso-bloody-lutely perfect!' I yell, before making a run for the bedroom and the cotton wool.

*

Shamed by my childish behaviour, and hugely relieved to see no sign of allergic reaction, I go back through to the lounge to make amends. I walk in on Bruce and Bill kissing on the sofa. They notice me so I can't just make a quick exit back the way I came. They're cool about it, which only highlights my acute embarrassment. Okay, so Bruce has inadvertently walked in on me mid-passion on the sofa more times than I care to remember, but I'm not used to being the one doing the walking in. Makes me feel very single. Not for long, I hope. In fact I vow here and now that I'm going to subject Bruce to walking in on me and Stelios during the raunchiest moment possible. I'll time it perfectly. I'll just have to seduce Stelios on the cushions in time for Bruce coming home from an afternoon cycle.

I grudgingly sit down in the armchair for ten minutes and chat nicely with them. I tell Bruce that it was Stelios on the phone, and that it's probably not considered rude to phone somebody at this time in Mediterranean countries. Bruce says that I'm probably right, and a truce is reached. I finally head for bed. Bill has taken his shoes off and nobody could say that I can't take a hint.

I get comfortable under the covers. But instead of mentally preparing for all eventualities at tomorrow's interview, I find myself worrying that Bill is going to stay the night. Not that I have anything against Bill staying the night. It's just that my bedroom shares a wall with Bruce's and I'm not too thrilled at the thought of hearing every squeak of Bruce's single bed. (Or any other kind of squeak, for that matter.) I'm still awake at half past two to hear the front door close quietly. Bruce is whistling.

CHAPTER TWELVE

Despite the fact that Caitlin's hair disaster had a happy ending, I can't help feeling a bit nervous about going to Pierre's today. But I've trusted him since I first came to London, and he only squeezed me in as a big favour. He likes the sound of Stelios and wants to do his artistic bit to make sure that Cupid's arrow hits the mark. And he *is* only putting my hair up, after all. 'Ciao, Bella!' Pierre calls as I walk into the salon. Someone once told me that he was actually born in Watford, but I've never dared ask him about that. He likes to perpetuate his cosmopolitan European image, and peppers his vocabulary with his stock repertoire of Italian and French phrases. (It's not clear which nationality he claims as his own, probably liking aspects of both: Italian shoes and French wine, or vice versa.) I gratefully accept a cappuccino and take the picture of the style we're hoping to achieve out of my handbag. (My *new* handbag. I found the perfect medium sized one in black silk with a Chinese embroidery detail on the corner, £19.99 from Warehouse.) Over the next forty-five minutes my hair is washed, conditioned, brushed, put in rollers, dried, combed, teased, sprayed, spritzed and speared with kirby grips. And then sprayed some more. I try not to open my eyes until it's completely finished. Partly because I want to get the full impact of the style, and partly to avoid being blinded. When I do look, it's not the same as the picture I brought. It's much, much better. It's perfect. I love it! Pierre is caught up in the magic of the moment, and kisses me on both cheeks before leading me round the salon and introducing me to four of his Ladies who Lunch. I'm reluctant to leave the warm, steamy cocoon of the salon. Feel like I could just sit in the corner and fall asleep to the soothing sound of Radio One muffled by the hairdryers. I know I didn't get enough sleep last night. Still, I should get used to this. TV presenters lead a gruelling life of late nights, early mornings and constant trips to the hairdresser. Pierre blows me a kiss as I leave, and calls out happily, '*Bonne chance!*'

At least it's not raining when I emerge. I check my watch. I've been consulting it every five minutes since I woke up. As if I'm expecting to be dragged through a time warp, or something, and lose a couple of hours. I'm happy to see that I've got plenty of time to get from here to WC1 for the appointment. I'm gradually learning London, postcode by postcode. The smell of car fumes combined with cigarette smoke and hot dogs is a bitter comedown after the thickly L'Oréal-ed air I've left behind. I decide to make an exception to my new rule and get a taxi. I'm out of practice at hailing cabs, but succeed in halting the ninth one I see. I hope it's a chatty driver. I'm in the mood for some conversation.

*

The taxi driver is really lovely. I hand him a £3 tip when we pull up in Berwick Square. He says that he's hoping to see me on the telly one of these days. His favourite programme is *Coronation Street*. ('Me and the wife never miss it. Even did the studio tour last summer.') I don't want to offend him by letting him know that I'm heading for more glamour and luxury than could be found in the whole of Manchester and its suburbs put together. I just smile professionally, and try to fit my hair out of the door without denting it (my hair that is, not the door).

Berwick Square is impressive. The overriding impression is one of uneconomical use of space and an abundance of clean, silver stone. The buildings all have plaques outside the doors. Most are bronze, although a couple are more modern, stainless steel jobs. I locate the one I'm looking for and then walk leisurely around the square about seven times. I don't want to appear too eager. Mind you, I don't want to appear flippant about the whole thing. I'm standing outside Shelbourne House fifteen minutes before the appointed time. My feet are killing me in these boots.

I don't like intercoms. They remove all possibility of making a dramatic entrance. It's the only way in though. I press the appropriate buzzer and after a short pause, a crackling voice instructs me to come in and take the elevator to the third floor. I can't be sure if it was Stelios or not. I try the door, but for some reason it hasn't unlatched. I really hate it when that happens. There's nothing for it but to annoyingly press the buzzer a second time. This time I'm pretty sure the voice doesn't belong to Stelios. 'Push the goddamn door, hard.' Open Sesame. I'm in. I'll just try and pretend that never happened. I want everything to go smoothly. I check my reflection in each of the three mirrors I pass. (It's a reflex action.) So far, so good. The carpet looks expensive. The walls are white and the paint work looks recent. There are fresh flowers everywhere. Lilies and irises and a regal arrangement of giant sunflowers (no chrysanthemums in sight). There's conveniently a fourth mirror in the lift. I discover that the building also houses a hair loss clinic, a contemporary jewellery designer's studio, a travel agency specialising in Scandinavian tours, and about six other companies, their business indiscernible from the nameplates. I'm always super-observant when I'm tense. Or terrified.

The big wooden double doors with the 'SIMPLY THE BEST' sign above them look foreboding. I knock extremely quietly before entering. They open onto a large reception room that probably made some interior designer a wealthy man. It's exquisite. More fresh flowers, an antique dark wood desk, prints of arrogant-looking race horses on the walls, a chaise longue and two matching sweetheart chairs in salmon pink and deep blue. There's a large coffee table from what I guess to be the same period as the desk, with copies of photography magazines fanned out across it.

It only takes me a millisecond to take it all in. It's Stelios I really want to concentrate on. I've been getting increasingly worried that I've built up the memory of him out of all reasonable proportion, and that I'll be disappointed to see him in the flesh. I needn't have worried.

He's leaning against the desk beside a man who must be Tomas. He stops talking and moves forward to greet me, kissing me on each cheek. 'Didn't I tell you, Tomas. Isn't she perfect?' I feel awkward suddenly. Tomas is looking at me as if I'm a shop dummy. His eyes move slowly up and down my body. He makes me wish I hadn't worn the skirt with the split. Too suggestive. Tomas is a wiry man, shorter than Stelios, with a much smaller build. His skin has a sallow, jaundiced appearance to it. He has a long moustache and small, dark bushy eyebrows, a hooked nose and unkempt curly dark hair. He finally looks me in the eye and seems to recognise his bad manners. 'Enchanted,' he says, holding out his hand to shake mine. He has chunky gold rings on almost every finger. Both men are dressed smart casual, as if they'd started the day in suits and discarded the jackets and ties in preference to comfort. He invites me to sit, and the three of us make ourselves comfortable, Tomas on one of the sweetheart chairs, Stelios and I on the chaise longue. I resist the urge to put my hand on his thigh.

Stelios gives me a brief description of the business. Explains how the office is just that, an office. Most of the filming is done on location, although they do have some rooms here which can be used for shoots. Post-production details are handled by an editing company on Wardour Street. He says that Simply the Best has never aimed for the mass market. That they don't want to make the mistake of becoming over-commercialised and, by doing so, compromise the standard of their work. He says they've seen too many of their colleagues make that mistake before. That must be the reason I'd never heard of the company until I met Stelios. It all sounds very impressive. I wish I could think of something interesting and astute to ask him, but he seems to have covered everything. I know that Stelios thinks I'm right for the job, but I have to convince Tomas as well.

Stelios stands up abruptly, and says that he's going to fix us some drinks. He walks through to a small kitchenette, more like an alcove in the side of the room. I can't see into it because the desk is blocking my view. Two seconds later, Tomas jumps up and joins him. They're talking in a foreign language that could be Greek or Egyptian. I'm too nervous to care. I wonder if there's a receptionist or secretary to handle the mundane paperwork. If so, there's no evidence of her today. Maybe she's on her lunch break. She's probably some ex-model who knows the video production business inside out and I decide to be grateful that there's nobody else here. I'm anxious enough as it is without having a blonde starlet around to intimidate me further. I wish that Stelios would come and tell me that everything's okay, and that Tomas thinks I'm great.

They reappear five long minutes later. Their manner is calm, confident and hospitable. I smile at Tomas hopefully, and he shoots me a lop-sided smile back. I suddenly remember that I've brought a CV with me, and pull it out of my handbag. It's only a bit crumpled. I hand it to Tomas with another smile, and tell him that he might be interested to read something about my background. That I studied drama at university, and had a summer job in a public relations company. I point to the 'Travel' section and emphasise the fact that I've seen much of Europe and have also been to Florida. He seems a little distracted, but nods and says that I seem to have a good education. I look at Stelios to see if he's going to put in a good word for me, but he doesn't seem to feel the need. He just passes me a glass. By the look of it and the smell of it, it's whisky. I hate whisky. I've hated it ever since a teenage party where I drank half a bottle of it mixed with Ribena and spent the whole night in the bathroom. I narrowly missed having to go to hospital to have my stomach pumped. Stelios clicks his glass against mine, and says that the drink is a tribute to Scotland. I don't want to appear fussy, or worse, like I've got no balls, so I take a big gulp and fight the urge to spit it all out. Tomas's glass is already half empty.

Stelios sits down beside me again. He takes one of my hands in his and strokes it gently. Like I'm a cat. He looks at Tomas as if for a cue, but

Tomas is on his way to get another drink. 'Kelly, my lovely Kelly,' he starts. 'This is a tough business. We may not be one of the big players, but even for us the competition is fierce. Tomas agrees with me that you are a beautiful young woman, but he is concerned that you do not have the experience to cope with presenting full-length videos. I disagree, and think, as I said before, that you will be a natural. As I also said before, I can make no decision alone. We must convince Tomas that you are right for us.' He squeezes my hand as he says this, highlighting the fact that he's on my side.

It suddenly hits me how much this job really matters to me. I panic at the mention of my not having enough experience. I've suffered too many rejections because of that, and I don't plan to suffer another if I can do anything about it. I'll do whatever I have to do to prove myself to Tomas. Everyone has to start somewhere. Even Anthea Turner. If I don't get a chance from someone, then I'm *never* going to get any experience. It's a classic catch-22 situation. I force my voice to appear confident, 'What can I do to convince him that I'm right for the company, Stelios? How can I *show* him I'm a natural?'

Stelios looks delighted that I've asked that question. I think he likes my spirit of initiative. He can see that I really care about getting this job. 'Well, Kelly,' he says slowly, 'Tomas and I were discussing that very same thing while I was getting the drinks. He thinks that the best solution is for the three of us to go through to another room and hold a kind of audition. We have a room arranged as a hotel bedroom, and we can make a short recording of you doing a makeshift presentation. I know you are not prepared, and I do not want to put you under pressure, but I think you can handle this. Think of it as your first screen test!' He laughs and looks at me questioningly. 'Can you do that for me, Kelly?'

Of course I can damn well do it. I've never been shy in front of a camera. I can waffle a bit about any old hotel and I can make it look good. Tomas rejoins us, and I tell him that I'll be happy to do a test run. He looks at me, and then at Stelios. 'I'll set up the equipment', he says, and disappears through a door behind me.

Stelios leans forward and kisses me lightly on the forehead. I start to feel dizzy. The video test is no big deal compared to that kiss. I'm not going to let lack of experience get in my way. Professionally, *or* romantically.

CHAPTER THIRTEEN

Stelios leads me through to the 'hotel bedroom' where Tomas is setting up a video camera on a spindly-legged tripod. This room is as plush as the rest of the place. There's a solid wooden double bed with a brilliantly white quilted bedcover over it. The colour scheme is the same as the reception room, with matching heavily draped curtains closed against the grey glare of the day outside. Stelios points out that the lighting conditions are fine for our purposes, but that it would take a lot longer to prepare for a genuine video shoot. He knows so much about this business and speaks with such authority.

Tomas stands back and nods to Stelios, which I presume means that everything's ready. Tomas is a man of few words and I don't like it much. The technical stuff may be ready, but what about me? I don't feel comfortable around people who guard their feelings so closely. Makes me feel like they've got something to hide. Still, Stelios trusts him and I trust Stelios. I really shouldn't be so judgemental. It's probably just an Egyptian thing. Stelios takes my glass and asks me to sit down on the edge of the bed and to make sure that my back is nice and straight. Tomas gets behind the camera. I can see a small red standby light above the lens. Stelios tells me that I should just say a few words about a hotel as if I were on a holiday programme. I figure I'll say something about the decor, mention that there's full room service and try to improvise for as long as they need. There are no flowers in here, but the air smells faintly of something not unlike baby powder. I'm suddenly hungry. I hope that my stomach doesn't start rumbling at a critical moment. I wish I could check my make-up again but I'll just have to trust in the power of my *Endure* foundation.

'Kelly, there is something not right with this picture. Try and relax some more. Do not think too much about what you are going to say. It creates lines on your forehead.' Stelios is talking and moving around me continuously, smoothing a crease from the cover, or pulling a tendril of hair away from my face. I wish that my hair was silky to his touch, but I know that it must feel crunchy under all those styling products Pierre used. God, I wish that Pierre could see me now. 'Lean forward a little, Kelly. Hold your chin higher, we do not want shadows in the wrong places.' Stelios has backed up against the closed door, and is squinting at the scene in front of him. He says a few words to Tomas, incomprehensible to me. The sound is guttural, and impatient. What am I doing wrong? I lift my chin another couple of centimetres higher. I just want to get started. I've managed to come up with some good phrases to throw in. Something about the 'opulent setting of Hampton House Country Lodge Hotel' (I like the sound of that) and that 'no attention to detail is spared, right down to the chocolate mint placed on the pillow every night'. I want it all to be over, the job mine.

Stelios approaches me again. 'Baby, it is too dark. We cannot see your face, and it is very important that we see your face. I think it is because of the dark colours of your sweater, no – what do you call it? Cardigan, I think. Take off the cardigan and we shall see what difference that makes.'

He called me *baby*! This is no time or place to start worrying about the transparency of the top I'm wearing underneath. I'm going to be professional and do exactly what they ask me to do. I pull it off, feigning indifference, and fling it onto a high-backed chair that's pushed against the wall.

Stelios smiles and starts fussing around with the bed cover again. His eyes are level with my nipples which are probably quite visible through my Gossard *Glossy* bra. I stare straight ahead. 'You know, Kelly, all our viewers are adults. I want to try something. Will you take off this other top you are wearing? And remove your bra. We are professionals here, and you must not feel shy in front of Tomas and I.'

I blink, and the thread of calm that I've been holding onto snaps. I look at Stelios. He's standing in front of me, holding out his hand helpfully to receive my top. Two things occur to me. The first is that this is *nothing* like Blue Peter, and the second is that I'm in a very threatening situation. I'm in a room with two grown men who seem to make the money to finance their lavish lifestyle from 'adult' films. I'm not *that* stupid. I finally understand that hotels probably don't come into it at all, except maybe to provide some variety in wallpaper and bed size. Seconds tick by, and I stare at the wall, praying pointlessly that Stelios is somehow joking, and that I can start my hotel speech now. A thought of my parents flashes into my head. My eyes flicker up towards his, and I know that he's serious. Frighteningly serious.

Before I can work out how to refuse, Stelios has leant forward towards me and taken hold of the thin fabric of my top. He's tugging it upwards, without saying anything. I feel tears well up in my eyes, and keep my arms pinned against my side. 'Come on now, Kelly. I know you will like this. What is the problem? Relax. Do not be so uptight. You can make a lot of money from doing this. Make a name for yourself. Make some contacts. Why fight it? I know you will be a natural. I will help you relax. Would you like that? I know you want me. I see it in your eyes. Do it for me.' Each phrase is punctuated by another tug at my top, each one progressively stronger. I feel one of the seams tear and am too scared to move. And too scared *not* to move. Before I can even think about what I'm doing, I bring up my right knee hard. I feel the zip of Stelios' trousers through my tights. And then I hear him shout words in Greek that I know you don't find in a holiday phrase book. His spit hits my face. He's still standing in front of me, one hand holding onto my upper arm painfully hard and the other protectively cupping the pain between his legs. 'Bitch,' he hisses, and tries to pull me down towards the bed by my hair. I inconsequentially remember the £18 I paid Pierre for the style. I feel like my hair's going to come out in his hand. He's still standing in a vulnerable position and all I can do is jerk my knee upwards again. It connects, and his grip loosens enough for me to pull out from under him and stand up shakily. As I do so, he rolls onto the bed. I'd somehow forgotten about Tomas in my panic, and am filled with a rush of fresh fear that he's going to prevent me from leaving. That they're going to combine their strength and make me do whatever they want. The stuff of fantasy when you read it in books but horror when you're facing the reality. I quickly look towards the camera but he's not behind it. The red standby light is still on. I place him a second later. He's leaning against an ornate mirror on the opposite wall, a smirk on his face. It's like he knew all along that I wasn't going to go for this, even if Stelios had confidently said that I was sure to be easy, willing to do anything to please him. Jesus Christ! Tomas is treating this whole thing like it's a big joke. Stelios is on the edge of the bed, his legs curled up towards his chest. I look at his face. His eyes are closed and he's mumbling in Greek. I notice what looks like the beginning of a cold sore on the corner of his mouth. I hope it's there for the rest of his fucking life. I finally see him for what he is, a manipulative, sleazy, heavy-handed piece of shit. My heart is beating fast and there's a sour taste in my mouth. I grab my cardigan, not taking my eyes off Stelios for a second. I move backwards towards the door. I guess that his pride's hurting him almost as much as his balls, but I want to be as far out of his reach as possible.

I make it out of the bedroom and stumble towards the double doors. I somehow think to stop and pick up my CV that Tomas discarded on the coffee table. It would disgust me to leave a record of my life in this place. I already feel violated, and know that I would hate these men to find the two, typed pieces of paper lying here as a tangible reminder of me. It's as if by removing the pages I can remove what's just happened. The tears are starting to cloud my vision and I throw the doors open and run. I don't wait for the elevator, but take the stairs instead. I become dizzy as I run down the seemingly never-ending, thickly carpeted steps. I don't remember leaving the building. I just find myself half-walking, half-running down a side street leading off Berwick Square.

*

It's only when I start thinking ahead as far as getting home that I realise I don't have my handbag. I fly through a mental list of what was in it. I'm terrified that there's something personal or sentimental that I've lost forever. From what I can recall I was only carrying £15 in cash, a powder compact, cigarettes, a Bic lighter and the magazine picture I'd taken to the hair salon. Nothing that I care enough about losing to make me consider trying to get it back. I wouldn't have gone back anyway, no matter what I'd lost in my flight. I know that it's going to be hard enough to just *think* back to that place, let alone actually *go* back.

But I still have to get home and I don't have anything. No money, no train ticket, no mobile phone. All I have is the cardigan, which I'm buttoning up clumsily as I walk, and the CV balled up in my fist. I notice that people are looking at me strangely, but walking past as if they haven't noticed me. I wipe some tears mixed with mascara off my cheek and push some strands of damp hair out of my eyes.

The fourth taxi driver that I ask agrees to drive me home and wait outside while I run inside for some cash. He looks dubious though. I don't even try to explain the mess I'm in. We drive towards home in silence.

CHAPTER FOURTEEN

I've spent the last three days in the safety of my own bed. Or it might have been four days, I've lost track. I've permanently crossed Cyprus and Egypt off my Possible Holiday Destinations list. I'm crippled by anger. Anger at Stelios for misleading me and tearing Caitlin's black top that I was wearing (among other things) but mainly, anger at myself for putting myself in a situation like that. I know I'm guilty of being gullible yet again. I sometimes see things in such a rose-tinted light that I'm incapable of thinking objectively. The words from last week's horoscope keep flashing in front of my eyes, the bit that said Aries people are '*determined to get where they're going by the shortest possible route and in the shortest possible time*'. I always convince myself that I'm going to get my big break by just being in the right place at the right time. I guess that only happens to a very small minority of the population and it's about time I accepted it. That's easier said than done. But I'm certainly not determined enough to get where I'm going by baring all, no matter what my horoscope says.

Bruce has been great. He was there to pay for the taxi and calm me down on Friday. He keeps repeating that it could have been a lot more serious if Tomas had got in on the act. That I did the right thing to resort to violence in order to get out of there. I'm so glad that I don't live alone. Just hearing Bruce making breakfast, watching TV and coming and going is reassuring. He never pressurises me to do anything. He says that if I want to stay in bed and get things straight in my head then he'll give me all the space I need. Luckily, he'll also give me hot buttered toast and the odd shoulder rub during my most pathetic moments.

I can't believe how much I've slept. I'll wake up, insignificantly look at the clock and go back to sleep. The most energetic thing I've done in these last few days is getting up to go to the loo and climbing back into bed again straight after. I can't be bothered to read, listen to music or move as far as the sofa to watch TV. I'm just so tired. I told Caitlin what happened and she was really cool about it. She came straight round after work on Friday and told me that I should press charges. But it's much easier to press my head under the pillow. I just want to put what happened behind me and write it off as yet another learning experience. I've learned so much from my mistakes recently that I'm expecting my invitation from MENSA to arrive any day.

One amazing thing that's come out of this is that I haven't had a cigarette for days and days. My body has been so numb with shock, anger and exhaustion that it hasn't noticed the lack of nicotine. (Or maybe it's the lack of nicotine that's caused the shock, anger and exhaustion.) It's weird because every time I've actually planned to stop smoking and made a conscious effort to quit, I've failed dismally. I don't have any cigarettes around to tempt me, and I don't really care. Bruce hates me smoking and always gets on at me about the trail of overflowing ashtrays I leave behind me. I suppose I could have asked him to get me a pack and he would have taken pity on me and got them, but it never really crossed my mind. It's early days, but the thought of less wrinkles in my forties is a cheering one. And I can stop buying that expensive smokers' toothpaste. Not that I can even remember the last time I brushed my teeth. In fact, I still have traces of last week's make-up on my eyelashes, and a few odd kirby grips that dig into my scalp when I lie down at a certain angle. It's so relaxing knowing that I'm not going anywhere and not having to spend hours in front of the mirror. Vanity can be hard work.

I haven't been taking any calls from my mother. Bruce can be relied upon to come up with a good excuse for where I supposedly am each time she calls. I can't bear to hear her say *I told you so*. Anyway, she'd probably overreact if I told her what happened and try every tactic in the book to get me to go home to Scotland. It's much easier to remain miserably in bed here than it would be at home. If I feel like spending a whole day in bed at home, I first have to come up with a good excuse such as having a migraine, or the onset of flu. I could never justify sleeping all day just for the sake of it. It's a strain trying to think up original ailments when I'm at home for any length of time.

*

It's hunger that finally drives me out of bed. I'm fed up of toast and need to stock up on some chocolate. I don't make much effort with my hair and make-up. I just make do with a rejuvenating shower and bung on a bit of mascara before putting my hair into a ponytail. I get dressed in a favourite pair of grey trousers and a comfortable baby blue sweater. Both could do with a wash.

Fluffy's missed me. I only have to run my nails along the bars of his cage a couple of times before he wakes up. Bruce has cleaned out his house and it now smells sweetly of sawdust. I'm convinced Fluffy recognises my voice. I give him some cucumber from the fridge and he stuffs it into his cheeks. The fridge is piled high with healthy stuff and therefore nothing that interests me. I don't know how Bruce survives on low fat yoghurt, couscous and salad. It's definitely time for me to have some culinary input around here.

Safeway's is the nearest supermarket and I could do with a trolley to lean on. Everything seems loud and hectic, cars roar by and unruly children push past me. It's only a ten-minute walk, but I'm tired by the time I get there. At least the supermarket's relatively quiet as it's the middle of the afternoon. The elevator music being piped out of the sound system is actually quite pleasant.

For once, I haven't made a list. I just plan to wander around aimlessly for a while and throw anything that appeals into the trolley. I bypass the fruit and veg section and find a few things I fancy in the next aisle. Banana yoghurt with chocolate crispies, herb and onion dip and a pack of four Milky Bar white chocolate mousses. Confusingly, I find myself in the toiletries section next and end up choosing a bottle of aromatherapy shower gel, some disposable razors and a can of deodorant.

I'm in the freezer section trying to decide between two different brands of microwave chips when I see Marjory. Busy Bees Marjory. She's got her hair done differently and is wearing a suit which looks like this season's Country Casuals. (I only recognise it because my mother's got one the same.) I don't feel up to small talk and am starting to move away in the direction of baking ingredients when she spots me. I wasn't sure if she'd even remember me but she apparently does. She greets me warmly and asks how the meal with my parents went. I smile and tell her that it was a lovely night. I can't help noticing the packet of smoked salmon in her basket. There's also a bag of lemons, a carton of double cream, a bottle of Baileys and some Belgian chocolates. Looks like she's not doing too badly for herself. I feel a bit self-conscious about the disgustingly unhealthy and unsophisticated heap of junk food in my own trolley, but she doesn't seem particularly interested. I'm just about to say a cheery goodbye and continue on my way when a concerned look crosses her face. 'Oh! I've just remembered. Maria at the agency has been trying to get in touch with you but nobody's answering the phone. Seems that the Visa people rejected your card. We've only got one of those old-fashioned credit card swipe machines in the office and it isn't the first time this has happened. Maybe there's been some sort of mistake dear, but I think you should give Maria a ring and clear it up.'

I assure her that I'll do so immediately and push my trolley into action. How absolutely embarrassing. I had no idea of the seriousness of my Visa debt, but I desperately wish I'd chosen to go to the corner shop and remained oblivious.

As I'm walking home I pass a scrawny-looking guy in an orange boiler suit and a matching cap. He asks me if I'd like a hot drink, and smiles winningly, adding hopefully, 'It's free'. I look him up and down and shake my head slowly. He's going to have earned every single penny of that £650.

*

I unpack the shopping bags on the kitchen table. I really went to town in the confectionery aisle. I shove a Kit Kat finger into Fluffy's cage and eat the other myself. Bruce gets home and looks at my purchases as if they've come from a different planet. He takes an apple out of the fruit bowl and cleans it on his shirt. I notice the pair of rather mouldy-looking pineapples on the breakfast bar and fling them into the bin. As soon as I've eaten some Pringles and herb and onion dip I think I'll do some cleaning. All this inactivity has made me feel like doing something and it's always satisfying to clean out the cupboards.

Liza from the recruitment agency phoned yesterday and I made the mistake of answering. She asked me if I could do Wednesday to Friday in reception at a publishing company in Chelsea Harbour. With lightening quick reflexes I told her that I couldn't because I was just on my way to get my wisdom teeth out. She sounded incredibly sympathetic. I felt terrible. Not terrible about lying but terrible about tempting fate like that. I hate going to the dentist. I have done ever since I was a child. My dentist was extremely tall and thin and his hands shook a lot. That's all I can remember about him really, but it later came out that he was a drug addict and was struck off the dental register. Who knows how many teeth he extracted in order to fund his habit? Doesn't even bear thinking about. And then there was the time Chris broke his front tooth on the edge of a swimming pool during a childhood holiday in France. It was a real test of my father's schoolboy French to understand the local dentist. I cried more than my brother did and have had what could safely be termed as a major phobia ever since. Anyway, I'm beginning to regret the lie. I can't phone the agency until at least Monday or it would look really suspicious, but I need the money.

*

I don't feel up to cleaning anything after I've finished eating. The Pringles led to microwave chips followed by another three Kit Kats. I only have the strength to make a quick list.

Tomorrow

Clean cupboards.

Phone Maria and tell her a cheque's on the way.

Let Fluffy out for some exercise.

Write to my grandmother.

Phone Caitlin and find out how dinner with Paul went.

Decide what to do about the mess my life's in.

CHAPTER FIFTEEN

A Get Well card arrives in the first post from the recruitment agency. As I read it I suddenly experience a stab of pain in a back tooth. Guilty conscience or giant cavity? I ignore the fact that it's peak time and give my mother a call. It's my birthday soon and I want to drop a few hints about a suede jacket that I saw in Kookaï last week. A jacket *is* practical and my mother might suggest that I buy it and offer to reimburse me for it as my birthday present.

She doesn't suggest any such thing. She's too excited about the news that the local minister has just run off with a librarian from Dundee. 'And she's young enough to be his daughter!' At least she doesn't remember to ask about the 'Simply the Best' interview. Although a part of me wishes she had, even if I don't want to talk about it. I'm compelled to know that what I do matters to my mother. I hope she's aware that I'm doing everything possible to get a permanent job, even if I haven't achieved anything yet that's worth boasting about to her friends.

I get around to cleaning out the kitchen cupboards after the phone call. Well, I say *cleaning*, but I use the word loosely. It actually involves taking everything off the shelves, throwing away anything that's more than six months past its 'best before' date and getting bored. I'll put the stuff back in the cupboards later. In need of a new challenge, I decide to clean out my handbag. I've been ignoring the furry pieces of chewing gum and stacks of useless till receipts for far too long. It turns into a fascinating chore. I sit down cross-legged in the lounge and end up wasting half an hour by reading all the receipts and piecing together my shopping history of the last three months. I appear to have bought more pairs of shoes, lottery tickets and bars of Galaxy than anything else, although there are a lot of receipts for Boots sandwiches. (And some of them the healthy ones in the Shapers range.) As I'm almost finished I find the lottery ticket with Lucy's phone number on it. There's a half-wrapped stick of Orbit stuck to it. I vaguely remember Declan telling me that she might have some work that I could help out with. I can truthfully say that I'm not doing anything today, tomorrow, or in the foreseeable future, and it might be a good idea to phone her.

Before I can put off doing it I pick up the receiver and dial the number. It's a mobile. She picks up after a few rings and I immediately get the impression that it's not a good time for her to talk. She says a breathless hello and then breaks off to speak to somebody in the background. '*No* Sonia, don't put the stick in your mouth. It's dirty. Throw it away and don't forget to wash your hands when we get back.' She comes back on the line and apologises for the interruption. She explains that she's taking some of the children she looks after out for a walk and wishes that she had an extra set of eyes on the back of her head. Although she sounds hassled, her voice conveys a sense of capability and humour.

I speak very fast, worried that I'll distract her and cause her to lose one of the kids. I explain who I am and tell her that Declan gave me her number and suggested I get in touch. That I'm not in work at the moment and could maybe help her out. That I'm not sure exactly what it is she does, but that I'd be very interested in hearing more about it. I stop to take a breath.

She laughs. 'I'm not sure I got all that, but I'd be happy to meet you for a coffee later when this lot have been taken off my hands.' She suggests the name of a coffee place and gives me directions. We agree on six o'clock. I like the sound of her and am looking forward to six o'clock.

*

I'm surprised when I look at the clock and see that it's already quarter to five. I've been engrossed in daytime TV closely followed by children's TV for the last four hours. Now I've got to get ready to go out and I still haven't dealt with the tins, packets and cans taking up every inch of the kitchen. I'm not sure what to wear. I certainly can't go out in this old skirt. I debate between a pair of tight black shiny trousers and a grey skirt that goes with my jacket with the fur collar. I settle on the grey skirt and put my hair up in a style which looks elaborate but actually only takes about twenty-five minutes to do. I grab my handbag, which is considerably lighter minus all the junk. Just before I leave I remember to phone the Busy Bees. Maria's not there (thank God) so I leave a quick, apologetic message on the answering machine telling her that I'll pop a cheque in the post tomorrow. As a last thought I scribble a message for Bruce and put it on top of a pyramid of tins of baked beans on the table:

B. Don't worry. The kitchen hasn't exploded – I'm just doing some spring cleaning. I'll sort it out later. The number for the pizza delivery people is beside the phone. K xxx

*

I'm ten minutes late arriving at the café. The tube stopped between two stations for ages, for no apparent reason. I can't help panicking whenever that happens, remembering vividly a horror book I read when I was far too young to be exposed to such things. A whole train full of people stuck in a tunnel get eaten alive by mutant rats. Nobody else seemed too concerned. Most of the other people on the train were on their way home from work, struggling unsuccessfully to keep their eyes open. And then it took me another fifteen minutes to find this place. I scan the small room and see a girl sitting on her own, reading something that looks like a children's textbook. It must be Lucy. I think she's about my age but she looks much younger. She's got reddish-brown hair scraped off her face by two combs (the kind I used when I was thirteen) and her skin is totally devoid of make-up. She's wearing a shapeless blue sweater that's gone all bobbly, and a pair of jeans. I feel hideously overdressed. She looks up and I wave. I'm already worrying that we'll have absolutely nothing in common to talk about and that this is yet another waste of time.

I sit down opposite her and apologise profusely for being late. I feel self-conscious about the elaborate eyeliner I so confidently applied earlier. Seeing Lucy's appearance I worry for the first time that my look is *too* much. She appears to be tired and I notice some splashes of brightly coloured paint on the backs of her hands. Her nails are very short. We spend a few moments chatting about the news that Declan's going to be a father. It's hard to believe. She tells me that she's known him since they were children. She's from Yorkshire but she used to spend a few weeks during every school holiday with her aunt in Ireland. Declan's house was nearby and they got together for a game of doctors and nurses or something like that, and they've kept in touch ever since.

I find that I'm genuinely interested in hearing about what she does. Her job might be exhausting, but she claims it's hugely rewarding and she doesn't ever get bored of it because every day is different. Nothing like an office. Some of the anecdotes she comes out with are hilarious, but she obviously takes her job very seriously. She runs a kind of play centre for children with special needs. Most are aged between four and twelve. None of the children live in special homes, they're all cared for by their parents, and the older ones attend special needs schools. A lot of parents are seemingly overwhelmed by the huge level of responsibility these children bring. They can leave their children at the play centre a couple of mornings a week and have some extra time for themselves, or to spend with their other kids. Lucy's done two degrees in London and is working on a third. A correspondence course in Developmental Disabilities, which she studies for whenever she can find a moment. When she asks me about myself, I find I don't really know what to say. Her life is so stimulating and selfless and I don't think she'd be interested in the crappy indecisions and frustrations of mine. I simply say that I'm tired of having no purpose to my life since I graduated. I don't really want to mention money in case she thinks that's all I'm interested in but I do throw in a quick comment about how I've been spending more than I've been earning in the last few months and that I can't continue in this way.

She tells me that she's in dire need of some part-time help, but that I can't be expected to know if I want to join the team without visiting the play centre to get an idea of what goes on. She says that if I like the set-up she'd be happy to welcome me on board five mornings a week. It's wonderful speaking to someone who tells it like it is. In the couple of job interviews I've had over the last six months, everything was so official; the interviewer at pains not to give anything away and risk losing their psychological advantage. I tell her that I'd be happy to come, and ask when's good for her. She says the sooner the better, so we arrange that I'll come along from nine until twelve tomorrow morning. With what I already imagine to be her customary bluntness, Lucy stands up and tells me she can't spend any more time sitting around nursing a coffee and rabbiting on about what she does. I insist on paying for the drinks and she gives me a slip of paper with the play centre's address on it. She tells me that if I get lost, anyone I ask will be able to point me in the right direction at Regent's Canal. I've appreciated seeing things through her eyes for the forty minutes or so we've been chatting. She may not look like the usual kind of person I hang out with (*that sweater?*) but she was a pleasure to talk to and I hope to be seeing more of her in the future. Being around her somehow makes me see how insignificant my own worries and complaints are. Just before she leaves she turns round and looks at my boots. 'Dress casual. High heels are useless when you're trying to round up six kids who are all running in different directions. And your clothes are invariable filthy after a few hours.'

I spend the whole journey home trying to figure out what I can find in my wardrobe that will be suitable. I think I've got an old pair of Levi 501s somewhere.

I phone Declan as soon as I get home to tell him that I took his advice. He's working late though, and I speak to Jenny. She laughingly complains that she hasn't experienced the so called 'glow' of pregnancy yet. Just a sore back and a rapidly expanding stomach. I commiserate, although the thought of my stomach rapidly expanding fills me with dread. I think I'll adopt. Anyway, she says she'll pass the message on to Declan and that they're both hoping we can get together soon. 'If we leave it much longer I won't be able to move – I'll be a beached whale!'

I spend the rest of the night putting away the kitchen stuff. I let Fluffy out to run around a bit but I'm constantly afraid I'm going to step on him. When I knock a pile of boxes of instant soup off the table I decide that it's just too dangerous and scoop him up and put him back into his cage. I give Caitlin a call and hear all about the glorious time she had with Paul. I try and concentrate, but it's difficult. I still haven't got around to finding those jeans for tomorrow. When I tune in again, Caitlin's saying 'his wife and him don't get on and he hasn't slept with her for eighteen months. I know that's what they all say, Kell, but I think he's telling the truth. He's just *sooo* wonderful. We're going to the cinema tomorrow night. He doesn't even mind seeing that new Brad Pitt film. He's great!' I know this isn't the time to come down all moral and warn Caitlin about what she's getting herself into. I should have done that in the beginning. I foresee tears in the future. Why does he have to be married? Well, at least Caitlin's happy for now. I'll be happy as soon as I find those bloody jeans and a pair of relatively low-heeled boots.

I still haven't had a cigarette.

CHAPTER SIXTEEN

I seem to be in the right place according to Lucy's instructions, but there's no sign of anything that looks remotely like a playcentre. I've already asked one old man who was out walking his dog. He just said 'this is it – Regent's Canal', and hurried away. Grumpy old sod. His big, black Labrador thrust its nose into my crotch before running off to catch up with is master. I *hate* that. All I can see is boats. Long ones with rooms inside and everything, like the ones further down at Camden Lock. I'm about to look for a payphone to ring Lucy for help when I see someone in the distance who looks familiar. I squint at the figure and walk a few steps closer. It *is* Lucy, and she's standing on the deck of one of the boats. It's painted a bright sunshine yellow, and as I get closer I can make out the name on the side, 'The Laughing Duck'.

'You found us,' she calls as I get within shouting distance. I can't believe it. I was expecting a little terraced playschool with a gate across the path, and pictures of animals stuck all over the windows. Actually, there are pictures of animals stuck to the windows of the boat. I notice three crepe paper ducks, a couple of frogs and a slightly deformed swan. I'm amazed and overwhelmed by what a great idea the boat is.

'You look surprised,' Lucy notes. 'What were you expecting? A bus?' I laughingly remind her that she never actually mentioned she was also the captain of a thirty-foot boat. 'I presumed Declan had told you. Anyway, now that you've found it, climb aboard.'

There's a gently curved ramp from the footpath onto the boat. I immediately notice the safety features that Lucy's added. The railing, both on the walkway and around the entire boat, is much higher than I've seen on the other boats. A strong iron mesh is fixed from the top right down to the deck. As I step on board Lucy explains that the boat was originally used for transporting timber along the Trent and Mersey canal. It was bought by a collector and brought down to London but after doing a lot of work on it he'd had some health problems and put it on the market. Lucy was looking for permanent premises at the time but was unimpressed by all the places she'd seen. And by the enormous monthly rent they were all asking. She had the idea of buying a boat when she remembered the fantastic family holidays she'd enjoyed as a child on the Norfolk Broads. Her father helped her find The Laughing Duck (formerly The Liverpool Lass) and the lottery grant helped on the financial side. 'And the rest,' she says with outstretched hands, 'is history.'

I can hear a lot of noisy chatter and banging about coming from inside and suddenly feel a bit nervous. I don't have any experience in this kind of thing, and I take the opportunity to ask Lucy how many children are here today. She says that there are eight at the moment. 'There should be nine, but Louise is having one of her bad days.' I find out that there are two other helpers: Doris, who's a retired primary schoolteacher, and Wendy, who's halfway through her nursing degree. 'They're all working on making peppermint creams for the kids to take home to their parents. The place was a sticky mess the last time I saw it so God knows what it'll look like now.' Before we climb down the stairs, which have been modified and include a wheelchair lift mechanism, I ask Lucy what kind of problems the children she takes care of face. I'm not sure what to expect, guessing that dyslexia might be a common one.

'Well, we've got Tara, who's been diagnosed with profound hearing loss caused by frequent bouts of otitis media as an infant – that's middle ear infection. And there's David. He has Down's Syndrome. Amanda: she's adopted and was born with what's recently become known in the States as FAS – Foetal Alcohol Syndrome – as well as having cerebral palsy. And Sonia, who's autistic. Those are the children that I know best because they've been coming here the longest. There are often new visitors. Today we've also got Karen, William, Jill and Lauren. I'll have to get a bigger boat! Don't worry,' she says, putting a hand on my shoulder, 'I know you'll never remember half of what I've just told you. It's much easier when you get to know the faces and the different personalities. They just need a lot more attention than your average child.'

Before I've even been introduced, a small boy, who I guess to be David from his distinctive features, runs up to me and throws his arms around my legs. He can't be much older than five. I feel a bit embarrassed. I'm not sure how to react. I haven't had much practice with children. I give him a smile, and self-consciously ruffle his thick dark hair. I am so glad I took Lucy's advice on the clothes situation. David's hands are covered in a gooey mixture of icing sugar and water. He says something which I can't understand at all. The grey-haired woman with her hands in a mixing bowl introduces herself as Doris. 'David's telling you that he's making sweeties. He says he's going to give you one.' I look down at David and tell him thank you. He doesn't loosen his grip on my thighs.

Lucy steps up to the table where the children are working and asks David to go back to his seat so he can finish making the lovely peppermints. He does as he's told and I notice in dismay the trail of white he's left across the front of my jeans. Lucy claps her hands and says that she's got a friend she wants everyone to meet. I watch the girl who must be Wendy translating everything Lucy says into sign language. I have my first close insight into the basic problems that people with disabilities are up against. I make a mental note to learn sign language.

Lucy tells everyone that my name is Kelly, and asks them to say Hello. There's a confusion of shouts and noises as they respond. I smile and give a kind of half-wave around the room. Lucy is explaining how I want to meet them all and join in their activity time when I see a flash of brown out of the corner of my eye. There's a loud clatter as the wooden spoon falls to the ground. I expect Lucy to start shouting but she simply picks the spoon off the ground and continues talking. It becomes impossible to hear her though because the little redhead (I'm pretty sure she was the one who threw the spoon) has started banging her palms against the tabletop. Doris approaches her and I overhear her saying, 'Are you bored, Sonia? Let's have a look at the dinosaur book for a while. It's your favourite.' The noise stops.

My three hours on The Laughing Duck feel more like three days. It's not that I hate it or anything, I'd much rather be here than in any damned advertising agency, but it's a constant strain to take in everything that's going on. I can see how Lucy would appreciate some extra help, but I feel horribly unqualified to make much difference. I had the chance to talk to Doris and Wendy for a few snatched moments at snack time, and they were very reassuring. They said that it's always a bit overwhelming when you're first in a group situation like today's. They explain that the afternoon groups are much smaller so that individual educational needs can be met, but that the mornings often turn into a free for all. 'As soon as you've started helping someone with their juice, another one will need the loo,' Doris says. 'It's a case of doing as much as you can without giving up and banging your head against a wall. Believe me, I've felt like doing that myself a few times!'

I leave as the parents start arriving to collect their kids. Lucy takes a moment to see me off. 'I know that everything was completely new for you today, but the children seemed to feel comfortable around you, especially David. He's a funny one. Adores Doris but usually just walks right past Wendy as if she isn't there. It's more helpful than you know just having an extra pair of hands around. How do you feel about coming back tomorrow, same time? If you decide to make this a regular thing I can pay you weekly. I can only manage £110 for five mornings which I know is peanuts, but if you're not doing anything else at the moment you might gain something other than a big salary from doing this.'

I'd rather have some time to think about the offer, but I don't know a tactful way of saying it. I really admire Lucy's drive and enthusiasm. I know that I could never match it, especially at nine in the morning. I put a brave face on though, and tell her that she can expect me tomorrow. She hurries back inside when a shoe comes flying out of the cabin door. It's a miniature Nike.

I'm mortified about getting the tube considering the mess I'm in but nobody pays me much attention. I'm relieved to get home and jump into a scaldingly hot shower.

*

Bruce was out on his bike when I got back but he turns up in the middle of *Home and Away*. He looks extra happy. I start describing my morning to him but stop when I notice him waving a blue air mail envelope around. He's like a kid with a new toy and I feel obliged to ask him who it's from.

'It came this morning from Tyrone. He's coming to London for a month or so and wants to know if it's okay to stay here. You don't mind do you? He can use the fold-down bed in my room, might even throw in a bit of rent money. He's a great guy. You'll love him. He's a photographer, wants to make some English contacts. I've known him for years.' When I get the chance to get a word in I tell Bruce that of course I don't mind his mate staying, but I can't help thinking that it could cause trouble in paradise.

'What about Bill? I thought the two of you were a pretty hot item?'

'Bill's cool about it. I've already rung him and explained the situation. We trust each other. Isn't it great? Tyrone can bring me heaps of pressies from my mum. And some Vegemite. And another cool thing is that he's arriving on your birthday. He can join in the celebrations!'

What celebrations? I'm not exactly counting the hours until I turn twenty-five. Still, Bruce's happiness is infectious. It's not often he gets this excited about something. He's usually unshakeable. I go through to the kitchen and make us celebratory milkshakes and Bruce goes to his room to rummage around for a photo of Tyrone that he's sure he's got somewhere and is dying to show me. After ten minutes he gives up and tells me I'll just have to wait 'til I meet the real thing.

CHAPTER SEVENTEEN

I spend the morning making a Nature Table, watching *Teletubbies* videos and building Lego animals. It's far more stressful than it sounds. I feel very comfortable (if a bit humbled) around Lucy, Doris and Wendy, but I'm still unsure of the kids. I'm okay one-on-one, but when I look around the room and see all those little pairs of hands getting into as much trouble as they possibly can, I panic. How does that woman in America who had the seven babies cope? Multiple nannies?

I'm flattered that Lucy wants me to come back next week. It's good to feel useful, even if I spend most of my time following one of the other helpers around asking what I should be doing. I did have a breakthrough moment today when Wendy taught me a few words in sign language and I was able to have a very basic conversation with Tara. I made her giggle at my mistakes. She signed to Wendy that she thought I was 'funny and pretty'. Those words aren't yet in my vocabulary and I was touched when Wendy passed on the message. They say children are more honest than adults. I'm greatly relieved that I can still look good with bits of twigs and moss in my hair. (Courtesy of William who got overexcited at the Nature Table.) I don't want to get too much into this 'natural look' and end up getting mistaken on the street for a lesbian Greenpeace reactionary, but I'm definitely beginning to understand the practicality of jeans.

*

Friday afternoon always has that good feeling about it. I go for a wander round Kensington Market. It amuses me to see that there's still an obvious demand for the kind of Indian skirts and cheesecloth tops that I practically lived in as a student. And the tubs of second rate one hundred percent vegetable hair dye in rainbow colours that I used to upset my parents by experimenting with. (You have to be careful when you go out in the rain after using that stuff.) It's like a walk down memory lane. Thank God I've developed my fashion sense since those days. I look back in horror at the bad hair year I went through when I was nineteen. In one particularly repulsive photo I'm standing happily beside Chris on a visit home, thinking I look great, resplendent in a patchwork mirrored skirt and a hand-knitted black mohair sweater. My hair is neon orange. Crayola neon orange.

I stop for a healthy drink in one of those trendy new juice bars. The kind of place where they liquidise granola and gooseberries and claim that it will keep you energised all day. My 'Big Buzz' (carrot, wheatgrass, root ginger, ginseng and royal jelly) *is* actually quite refreshing – a lot like Slush Puppy, which I've always adored. But pricey at £2.95. I sit around for a while trying to work out if I feel energetic but I don't stay too long because it's no smoking in here. I've decided to just have the odd cigarette when I'm relaxing and stuff. I don't think it's too bad for you if you smoke less than ten a day. And when I'm in my forties I hope to be able to afford plastic surgery anyway. A Cher face-lift would be nice. Or maybe a Goldie Hawn job.

I stop by Caitlin's office at five-ish. I know she's got another hot date with Paul later but I haven't seen her all week and want to have a gossip. Not that I've got much to gossip about. The only scandals I've witnessed in the last few days are spotting an old man nicking a packet of rice from Safeway's and breaking up a fight between two under-fives. But I also want to show off the stunning stainless steel ashtrays I got in Urban

Outfitters. I threw away all the ashtrays in the flat last week, in a moment of insanity.

When I get to Caitlin's desk there's no sign of her. Her assistant Becky helpfully explains that she went to the bathroom to get an eyelash out of her eye, adding dubiously, 'but that *was* twenty minutes ago.'

I find Caitlin in front of the mirror, clutching a tub of hair wax in one hand and a bottle of *Joop!* in the other. The air is suffocating – Right Guard deodorant, I think. She's happy to see me. 'Enough eye shadow? Too much blusher?' I assure her she looks great. Paul is coming to the office to pick her up and she's worried that she doesn't know how to do that 'transforming your day look into an evening look' thing she saw explained on GMTV. She's a bit hyper and asks me three times if I think her suit looks okay. (Personally I think she should have gone for her grey one from Next, but I obviously don't tell her that.) I wish we were getting ready to go out *together*. It's been ages since we had a really good night out. Caitlin practically pushes me out of the door at five forty-five. She says that she *does* want me to meet Paul but that it's too soon to introduce him to her friends. And she's already decided that she's going to be frowning intelligently at the computer screen when he arrives. Something about not appearing too keen and presenting a responsible, mature, professional image. As I leave she's getting into position, practising a surprised 'Oh, I got so caught up in this report I didn't notice the time' expression.

I check out every man I pass on my way to the tube station. They're all either too old, too young, too thin, too fat, too pale, or are wearing shell suits. I get stuck in the rush hour and don't get home until seven. Bloody commuters.

I'm determined to enjoy my weekend since I'm now going to be working Monday to Friday. Even if it *is* just the mornings. I might try arranging something with Declan and Jenny, or seeing what Sarah's up to. I let Fluffy out to stretch his legs, and look about for the TV guide. I know it's around here somewhere. I'm sure Anthea's on the cover again.

*

I spend the rest of the weekend on my hands and knees. Unfortunately, it's not spent engaged in any perverse sexual acts. I succeeded in finding the TV guide but somehow managed to lose Fluffy. I got engrossed in a couple of game shows and when I remembered to put him back into his cage he was nowhere to be found. I searched absolutely everywhere, even in the toaster and inside every shoe in the hall cupboard. Bruce spent a few hours on Saturday afternoon helping and even Bill made a token effort. But *they* were able to just go out and have fun and forget all about Fluffy. They told me that he'd come out of wherever he's hiding when he's hungry. I, on the other hand, was filled with guilt and didn't stop looking until the early hours of Sunday morning when I just couldn't keep my eyes open any longer. I had awful visions of Fluffy being inside the Hoover the next time we turned it on. Or in the oven the next time Bruce or I decided to cook. If he'd been in either of those places, it could have been *months* 'til we found him.

By Sunday afternoon I'd got to the point of considering calling in the police with their sniffer dogs. I made one last ditch effort with the torch and almost had a heart attack when I came face to face with Fluffy's beady black eyes and twitching nose. He was under the fridge and had enterprisingly made a bed out of a shredded piece of kitchen roll and a collection of bits of food he'd found on the floor. It was quite a feast. I noticed a half-nibbled Rolo which I'm sure I dropped last month. (I only remembered because it was my last one and I was really annoyed at losing it.) Fluffy didn't even care about all the worry he'd caused me. He looked totally unrepentant. I put him in his cage and told him that he wasn't getting out for a week as a punishment. Then felt horribly like my mother and reduced it to three days.

*

I get around to writing a long letter to my grandmother, mentioning how expensive it is in London and pointing out that I'm living on cornflakes and digestive biscuits. Going by past experience this should induce her to either slip me a tenner in her next letter or send me a batch of her amazing syrup flapjacks. It's always tricky writing to grandmothers because you have to watch what you say. I don't mention my audition to be a porn star but go into great detail about The Laughing Duck. I'm sure it will appeal to her because my grandmother was a Wren during the war and has always urged me to go into one of the 'caring professions'.

I'm getting worried about my utter lack of a social life these days. Bruce is out again in one of those cool Soho clubs. I'm usually reluctant to go to those places because I'm terrified about getting turned away at the door. (Not that I ever give that as my reason for not wanting to go. I just complain about the poor selection of cocktails I've heard they have or something like that.) Some of them only let you in if you're wearing a dog collar and a cling film top, or get your hair cut by Nicky Clark. I spend a few hours stressing out about not being seen in any of the right places and missing countless opportunities to be in Hello magazine. Then I come up with the fantastic idea of having a birthday party. I haven't had a birthday party for years. A lot of birthday *pints* but nothing that would constitute a real party. This could be a real party. The kind that people are still talking about weeks after it's happened. Feeling suddenly inspired I start writing up the guest list. This, however, proves to be even *more* worrying. After twenty minutes I've still only got ten names on the list, and that's including me, Bruce *and* Doug from the grooming parlour. I suddenly remember that Bruce's friend Tyrone will be arriving on my birthday and add his name to the list. (I still can't take that name seriously. What were his parents *on* when they came up with it?) I've now got Caitlin, Paul, Bruce, Bill, Sarah, Declan, Jenny, Lucy, Doug, Tyrone and me. Five females and six males. But four of the guys are gay, one's married and the other is married *and* my best friend's boyfriend. I don't want my party to turn into an appreciation society for the IKEA catalogue. I'll have to come up with some more unattached, straight men soon. It's only a week 'til my birthday.

CHAPTER EIGHTEEN

I meet Caitlin for lunch on Wednesday and rope her into helping out with the party arrangements. I've already invited everyone on my original list for Saturday, the night of my actual birthday. Nine for nine thirty. I hate it when nobody turns up at a party until the pubs shut. They can all come, and Doug's bringing his new boyfriend Pete. Great – another gay man. Caitlin's not her usual self. Her eyes are glazed over and she can't concentrate on the Oddbins shopping list I'm working on. I've seen that look before. It's obvious she had great sex with Paul last night, but she hasn't said so in as many words. I grab the fork out of her hand before she can finish decorating the napkin with an indentation of her name entwined with his. Honestly, it's like she's fifteen again. Next thing I know she'll be ripping the page with his number on it out of the phone book. The least she can do is share all the gory details. She always used to. Just because he's a married man she's gone all secretive and grown-up. I bet he tells *his* mates about his 'bit on the side'.

We've decided to make it into a really mellow evening. Ambient music on the stereo, ultra-cool cocktails and dim lighting. (Anything to make that carpet less noticeable.) I refuse to consider making punch. Too reminiscent of student parties and too much hassle to find a bowl big enough. I haven't got very far in solving the glaringly obvious lack of suitable men problem though. Caitlin says that she's going to try and entice Ed from her office into coming. A bit unfair that one, because he's had a crush on Caitlin for the last six months and will obviously jump to the wrong conclusions. But all's fair in love, war and party planning. At least he's tall. Maybe I can give him a couple of Orgasms (the cocktail that is, at least to begin with...) and provide a shoulder to cry on. As long as I'm not the one crying I don't mind. There's always one girl crying at every party I've ever been to. You know, hogging the bathroom and telling her life story to anyone that gets in her way. (I know, *I've* been that girl.) Sarah said she'll do her best to bring along a couple of spare men. Lucy wasn't much help. Complained that she doesn't have the chance to meet any men after five days spent up to her eyeballs in play dough and five nights of hitting the books. By the weekend, she says that she doesn't feel generous enough to share her bed with anyone.

Caitlin asks me what I want for my birthday. We always used to surprise each other but it got a bit pointless when we realised that she was giving me exactly what *she* wanted and vice versa. Little gold earrings aren't my style, and I could tell that Caitlin didn't think much of the glittery showgirl eyelashes and marabou hair slides that I gave her last year. It's awkward though, demanding a present as if you've just been waiting for the chance to put in your order. 'Oh, nothing Cait,' I say virtuously. 'As long as you're there at the party and promise to provide moral support all night and not disappear into my bedroom with Paul.' She doesn't buy it though, and after a bit more pushing I admit that I'd love either the new Sheryl Crow CD or a silver-plated cigarette holder. (I saw a woman holding one in a black and white film on Sunday afternoon and it looked so sophisticated.) We then shut up on the topic of presents so that I can pretend to be surprised on Saturday.

My mother called last night and said that I'm getting past the age of big, fancy birthday presents. Asked me if I wouldn't prefer a hand with the council tax bill instead. As *if*! She said that she's got a couple of little things for me and that she'd put them in the post later in the week. I remind her to send them registered delivery and to get insurance if the value of the goods exceeds £500. She just laughed dryly. I'm still waiting for the pearl necklace she promised me for my twenty-first. For some reason I got a home office filing system instead.

A few birthday cards have already arrived. Makes a nice change from the usual assortment of bills and rejection letters. One from Sally in Greece (saying that it already feels like summer out there and that she's just got two new kittens), one from my Aunt Isobelle (can't actually remember what she looks like but she can't be bad because she included a £10 book voucher) and a couple of others from university friends. The problem is that all my friends are scattered around the world and therefore can't be included on the party list. It's not like I don't have enough friends or anything, just that I don't have enough friends within visiting distance. *Big* difference. I also got a national research survey thing in the post today. It says that if you take a few moments to fill it in you'll automatically be entered into a £5000 prize draw. Half an hour later I was still debating which bath and shower products I use most often. The choice was limited and I certainly wasn't going to tick the *shops' own brand* box. In the end I settled on Radox and moved onto the next tricky question, 'How would you best describe your hair/skin/eyes?' I was almost late for Lucy's but managed to run for once and arrived just on nine. Lower heels do have their advantages, although I never thought I'd hear myself say it.

I haven't done any food shopping for what feels like ages. I eat Cadbury's Mini-Eggs and a bunch of seedless grapes for dinner. It's not my fault if the Easter chocolate is already in the shops. It appears earlier and earlier every year. What's a girl supposed to do?

*

Liza from the agency phones at eight o'clock on Thursday morning. She sounds ridiculously chirpy for this time of day. Apparently Kathryn's got shingles. They need someone today and tomorrow, and possibly next week too. I try and put the right amount of sincerity into my voice when I tell Lisa that I'm terribly sorry but won't be able to manage it. I give her a rundown on my new job and tell her that I'd still be delighted to do any assignments she can offer between two and six in the afternoon. I tell her to send my best regards to Kathryn. I wouldn't have done it even if I *hadn't* been working at the play centre, though. There's no way I'm going to voluntarily work all day on the day before my birthday. I want to spend the afternoon getting ready to go out on Friday night. Liza doesn't sound so chirpy when she says goodbye. In fact she sounds a bit exasperated.

I'm half an hour late getting to the boat but it's for a good reason. David's been really miserable all week. He's been following me around pathetically for the last few days, but won't enter into any conversations or games, which everyone says is totally unlike him. I spent a lot of time trying to persuade him to tell me what's wrong. I'd almost got to the point of giving up when he finally decided to share what's been bothering him. It took me a few attempts to figure out what he was saying, and he was getting pretty impatient with me by the time I did. He just kept repeating 'moy gwo fish doy' and it took at least an hour for me to work it out. His goldfish died! I was practically jumping up and down in excitement when I finally understood, but David still looked just as miserable. I told him not to worry about it because I was going to bring him a big surprise. He looked at me with baleful eyes and asked, 'Bwing me chocwit?' I told him that it was going to be something much better than chocolate and he brightened up for five minutes.

So here I am, as promised, carrying a goldfish dangling in a plastic bag. Inflation is a terrible thing. I remember when I was a kid goldfish only cost fifty pee each. Now they're up to £3.85. David doesn't get dropped off until nine forty-five and the anticipation's killing me. I let Lucy in on my plan yesterday and she said that it was a nice idea but to check first with David's parents when they picked him up. I got a bit distracted though when I noticed Tara licking the TV, and it slipped my mind. Still, I'm sure they won't mind me spreading a little happiness. They've already got the bowl and fish food, after all.

As soon as David's coat's off, I hurry him over to a quiet corner of the activities room. (I don't want the other kids to think I'm into favouritism.) I've got an empty family size margarine tub ready and I make a big deal of hiding the bag behind my back. David looks confused and like he might start crying so I quickly present him with the goldfish. The look on his face is well worth the £3.85. He literally lights up, and thrusts out his hands to take the present. I show him the margarine tub, and tell him that I'll open the bag to let the fishy out. It plops into the tub and starts darting around frantically. David has his nose two inches from the water and is utterly captivated. I feel such a glow of pleasure. Just then, our new girl, Rosalind, starts shouting and I look over and see her hitting Sonia hard across the head. Sonia starts screaming. Doris and Wendy are already helping kids go to the toilet, and Lucy's up on deck talking to some parents. I rush over to the girls and haul them apart. I tell William (in no uncertain terms) to play nicely with Sonia, and set up Rosalind at the table with a book about rabbits. I'm beginning to know how to cope in this kind of situation. Just takes a bit of quick thinking. I remember David, and head back to where I left him. But something's wrong. David's staring out of the window at a man on a bike cycling along the footpath, and doesn't seem to notice me. The margarine tub is empty. Well, the water's still there, but THE GOLDFISH IS GONE.

Oh my God! David has eaten the fish. His parents will sue. I'll go to prison. How am I going to tell Lucy? I kneel down in front of him and prise open his mouth, entertaining horrible visions of seeing an orange tail disappearing down his throat. No sign of it though. I look into David's eyes. 'Where is the fish? *Where* is the fishy, David?' My natural instinct is to start yelling but I don't want to scare the kid, get the attention of the others or alert Doris and Wendy to the disaster I've allowed to happen. Maybe I should just pretend *nothing's* happened. The bag's in the bin, and nobody actually saw me coming in with the fish. Except David. Help! What if it's still swimming in his stomach? Maybe I should rush him to Accident and Emergency for an X-ray. I notice Lucy coming down the stairs and try not to catch her eye. I grab a nearby book about trains and try to make it look like we're using the reading corner for legitimate purposes. I put on a singsong voice and try to make a joke out of it. 'Where's that naughty fishy, David? Where's he hiding?' I make a show of opening a few drawers and saying 'nope, not in there'. David has started to giggle and finds the whole situation highly amusing. He starts banging his arms against his body and laughing even louder. Suddenly, the excitement becomes too much for him, and I notice a large wet stain spread across the front of his blue corduroy trousers. We've got a cupboard full of surplus clothes in case of emergencies like this. I put the fish problem to the back of my mind and head for the cupboard. I can't leave him in those wet clothes.

I get David through to the boy's bathroom. He's beginning to grizzle and it's difficult to keep him amused. As I start to pull down his trousers he suddenly remembers something. 'Fishy!' he shouts. I wish he'd keep his voice down. I start to tug at his trousers, my thumbs in the pockets. He starts to giggle again and a moment later I feel something slimy in the left pocket. Oh my God. I think I've found the goldfish. I tell David to close his eyes so the fishy can find a hiding place and then we'll play hide and seek. He does as he's told, a big smile on his face. Quick as a flash I retrieve the slightly squashed, motionless fish from his pocket and fling it down the toilet, trying not to think about what I'm doing. He opens his eyes just as the toilet's flushing. I plaster a big smile across my face and finish the clothes change. After washing our hands I suggest we go and play with the sand. I exhaust myself for the rest of the morning, trying to keep David distracted. As his mother is putting his coat on I hear his little voice saying 'Where's Fishy, Mummy?' His mum gives him a quick hug and reminds him that his goldfish is in heaven.

CHAPTER NINETEEN

March the 29th. When I wake up I'm extremely groggy and my mouth feels like it's coated in the synthetic fuzzy stuff that Fluffy makes his bed out of. I can't remember much about last night. Only that Caitlin and I got round a lot of bars and that we broke one of my cardinal rules and took a minicab home. Even worse, we didn't go to a minicab office but just accepted a drive home from one of those touts who hang around outside clubs and make up the fare off the top of their head. It's usually in the region of £14 regardless of whether you're going to East London or Ealing Broadway. The last thing I remember is the enormous black driver telling us that he hated his job and how he wished that he had a girlfriend to go home and make sweet love to. We were lucky, he was just a manic depressive. Could have been a psychopath or anything. Oh my God! I'm twenty-five! It's my birthday. Shit, it's not the same when you get a bit older and can't go running through to your parents' bedroom where a shiny new bike with stabilisers awaits you. I could do with some stabilisers in my life right now.

I jump out of bed and give Caitlin a gentle kick. Must have been harder than I thought because she wakes up very quickly and 'Happy Birthday' is not the first thing out of her mouth. I climb around the fold-down bed and go to pick up the mail.

There's a few more cards and the package from my mother has arrived. It doesn't look like it's pearls. I take everything back to bed and rip open the paper like a kid. Caitlin's watching through one eye. It's a book. It's just a *book*. It's not even a book with a positive, loving message. It's that bestseller, 'The Rules'. The one that teaches you how to find a husband by: (a) never being available for a date at less than three months notice; (b) learning everything there is to know about your loved one's interests, even if that includes fly-fishing; and (c) not sleeping with him until after the church service. (Actually, I'm not sure about that last one, but it seems to fit in with the general gist of the book.) I'm just preparing to never speak to my mother again when something else drops out. It's a voucher for a full body aromatherapy massage in the beauty salon in Harrods. She *does* still love me! Caitlin is green with envy. (Or maybe that's just the effects of last night's tequila.) I can't help feeling happy on my birthday. There's also an excellent card from Chris. On the front is a picture of a completely moth-eaten cartoon mouse wearing white gloves. Inside it says, 'Mickey without make-up'. There's also a hugely generous cheque for £50. It's at times like this I don't mind so much that my little brother has got a great job with great prospects before I have. There's also an official looking envelope. It'd be great to get a job offer as a birthday present. No such luck. It's a rejection from the over-fifties holiday company. The old farts.

Caitlin grudgingly gets out of bed, stumbles over and gives me hug. I don't even mind that she's wearing my best camisole top to sleep in. She rummages in her bag and produces a small gift in gold wrapping paper with matching ribbon. I open it immediately, trying not to remember the cigarette holder I asked for. Wow! It's beautiful. It's long and silver and exactly like the one I saw in the film. Where on earth did she find it? And not only that, there's also a matching compact filled with my favourite shade of translucent face powder. I hug her tightly until she extricates herself and says that she's desperate to pee.

Bruce is already up and hands me a box-shaped present. 'No more hamsters, I'm afraid,' he says as he kisses me on the cheek. I don't know whether I should hit him or strangle him when I discover the brand new Grow Your Own Magic Garden kit. When he tells me that there's also a bottle of Veuve Clicquot in the fridge I can't bring myself to hit him. I tell him that he can be the first to taste the garden when it's ready. But that *I'll* be the first to try the champagne.

I also get a Boots voucher from my grandmother, a card from an ex-boyfriend in New England (there's a picture of a bison on the front – should I take that to mean anything?) and a card from Declan and Jenny saying that they're looking forward to the party. Oh my God, the party! It's in less than ten hours. I start making a list of what to do but Caitlin forces the pen out of my hand and insists that we watch some Saturday morning children's TV before we do anything that involves thinking. I'm interrupted twice by happy birthday phone calls from my parents and my grandmother. I keep the conversations short and sweet.

*

Caitlin goes home at about four and I go out to buy a few last minute bits and pieces. A couple of times I get the urge to tell someone that it's my birthday but I resist. It would be a good line to use on sexy men. I could invite them to the party. But I don't see any sexy men in Marks and Spencers so I give up on that idea.

Bruce moves most of the furniture from the lounge through to the back of the kitchen and double checks the booze supplies. I put Fluffy into my room, worried that somebody will think it's a good idea to let him out to play. Bruce is a bit overexcited about Tyrone's arrival. He keeps running to find the letter and double check the plane's arrival time. He's told Tyrone to get a taxi from Heathrow which will cost a fortune but it's worth it not to have to get on and off trains with luggage. Tyrone's due at about six and Bruce and I spend the next fifteen minutes fighting over the bathroom. I say that I should go first because I take much longer to do all the stuff *after* the shower whereas for Bruce it's *just* a shower and he's ready to go. It's my birthday and I win. Bruce is still explaining about all the time it takes for him to style his hair and find a clean pair of socks when I close the bathroom door behind me.

I haven't actually had many parties before. I usually prefer to go to other people's so I'm free to leave as soon as I decide I don't like it. I hope that other people don't think the same way. I'm not going to do a buffet or anything but I have to serve *some* food. I was totally against the idea of crappy little bowls of nuts and crisps. They'd destroy the image completely. I therefore felt quite justified in splashing out on a couple of sushi selection trays from M&S. Even if nobody likes sushi they still *look* good. Sushi's very fashionable again.

I don't want to dress up too much. It wouldn't feel right to get all tarted up just to sit in my own lounge, even if it is my birthday. After much deliberation I've decided on my favourite grey trousers. That's the beautiful thing about them; they're fine for the supermarket *or* for a party. My only concession to the occasion is a new fitted lambswool cardigan in fuchsia pink. I found it in Marks and Spencers on my way to the food hall. If you can pay for something like that with your potatoes then it doesn't feel extravagant at all. More shops should do it.

Bruce phones the airport to see if Tyrone's flight is on time. He's devastated when they tell him there's a four-hour delay. I tell him not to worry because the party will just be getting into full swing by that time. He cheers up a bit and starts putting some glasses of Sex on the Beach onto a tray and into the fridge. God, that brings back good holiday memories.

Caitlin phones at seven to ask for the millionth time if I think it's a good idea to bring Paul. 'What if someone recognises him? Have you thought of that? He *is* married you know, even if he doesn't sleep with her.' I tell Caitlin to stop being so paranoid. It's not like he's Elvis Presley or anything. She finally agrees and tells me that she's meeting him for a drink at eight and they'll do their best to get here by nine. I need Caitlin around when the first guests arrive to give me some moral support and to tell me that my make-up's okay.

*

Caitlin's on time and I finally get to meet Paul. I like him as soon as he says '*Bonne Anniversaire*' and gives me a bottle of white wine. French, of course. I wish that I could meet a suave foreign man too. He's not really Caitlin's usual type though. He looks far more intelligent than most of her ex-boyfriends. More brain than brawn for a change. We sit down in the lounge and I remember to light a few scented candles to add atmosphere. Every time Caitlin and Paul look at each other I'm terrified they're going to start snogging and I'll be sitting here like a spastic, talking to myself. She's behaving herself though, and as soon as Bruce comes through and he and Paul have been introduced we nip up to my bedroom for a double vodka and lime, a gossip and a last minute make-up inspection. (We tell the boys that we're just going to check on the paper napkins. Men are so thick.) Ed can't bloody come. He's up in Cheshire visiting his parents.

The vodka calms my nerves and I start thinking it won't really be so bad if nobody turns up. We can watch *Die Hard 2* which I'm sure I noticed in the TV guide is on tonight. The video's still not working so we can't record it. The thought of the video reminds me of Sarah and how much I'm looking forward to seeing her. It's been *weeks*. After another preparatory vodka I'm wondering if Sarah and I should do our *Walking On Sunshine* routine. This is going to be a great party.

CHAPTER TWENTY

Declan and Jenny arrive just after nine thirty. Jenny's stomach *is* pretty big. They give me a selection of Body Shop stuff, which always comes in useful. I'm glad they're here. They make the lounge look more full. It's always tricky at the start of the night. I'm relieved that I'm already half-pissed. Declan and Paul look like they've hit it off and start a very boring conversation about street layouts in Guildford as opposed to those in Marseilles. Jenny starts saying something about not being able to drink, 'what with the baby and all', but I take no notice and thrust a Sex on the Beach into her hand. Bruce is on the phone to the airport again.

Bill, Doug and Pete arrive next. I'm not sure if they all came together or just met up on the front path. Doug and Pete certainly look very *together*. I pretend not to notice Doug biting Pete's ear as they come through the door. Doug gives me a selection of brightly coloured ribbons as a present but I can't help thinking they were actually destined for some pampered pooch. Pete gives me a packet of Marlboro Lights. Now *that's* a handy present. Bill makes a beeline for Jenny and immediately puts his hand on her stomach. 'Is it kicking yet?' he asks, in seemingly genuine fascination. When Lucy turns up I'm a bit worried about what she'll make of the gathering but she doesn't seem too fazed. She's brought a batch of chocolate brownies which I'm ecstatic about.

Even more so when she warns me that they're pretty powerful thanks to the quarter of skunk she's added. Somehow this surprises me. I always think of Lucy as being so wholesome. Still, I don't suppose it makes much difference as long as she doesn't attempt to look after those kids when she's stoned.

Sarah and I do the whole screaming, jumping up and down and throwing our arms around each other girlie thing when she arrives. She's brought Neil and Ben ('guys from work') which I'm pleased about. Adds a frisson of tension when there are fresh men around. I take their coats through to my bedroom, checking the labels as I go. The one that belongs to the shorter bloke is from Debenhams, but the other one's is Dolce and Gabbana. Very interesting.

I give up hovering around the door when the novelty of the frequent doorbell ringing wears off, and go to find a seat in the kitchen. It's already filling up with people as kitchens at parties invariably do. I have a glass of champagne in one hand and a Black Russian in the other. There's a lot of noise and people laughing and I take this as a good sign. I'm feeling very relaxed about this party thing. I take a sip of the champagne followed by a sip of the cocktail. I alternate between the two for the next five minutes until both glasses are suddenly empty. As soon as my hands are free I light a fag and close my eyes.

My little piece of personal calm is rudely shattered a few minutes later by Caitlin's arrival at my side. Her face is completely white which does *not* do good things for her eye make-up. She looks like she hasn't slept in three days which is bad considering we only had the one rough night. I get a serious feeling I don't want to hear what she's about to say. Everything was going *so* well. She starts speaking in this urgent, melodramatic stage whisper and I have to lean forward a few feet to hear her. (I narrowly miss falling off my stool at the breakfast bar.)

'I told you this was a stupid idea. Your bloody friend Sarah has just walked straight up to Paul and asked him how Claudette is. *Claudette*! I didn't even know her name before and now I'm at a party with a woman who's probably his wife's best friend. Paul was really quick, and introduced me as someone he's working with. Come to think of it, I *am* someone he's working with. But we were holding *hands*. What's that bitch Sarah going to think?'

I can see two Caitlins, swaying in front of my eyes. I don't know what I'm meant to be saying. 'Sarah's not a bitch,' I try. Nope, wrong answer.

'For fuck's sake, the least you could do is give me some advice. It's your fault that Paul's here in the first place. It's *your* bloody birthday. *You* persuaded me to bring him. We'll have to leave, but we can't leave together. Too suspicious. He'll have to leave first and wait down the road for me, then I can say I have a terrible headache. You back me up. Say something like "Shit, not one of your killer migraines", and then I'll leave, find Paul and we'll go into hiding in a nice anonymous hotel room.'

I know that I'm going to have something very bad to deal with tomorrow but I just can't whip up any sense of urgency at this precise moment. Sarah's not a bitch. I love Sarah. Oh God, the room's starting to spin and it's only half past ten.

*

I guess that half an hour or so must have passed and I'm in the lounge getting talked at by the Dolce and Gabbana guy. On closer inspection I really don't like his teeth or the mole on his upper lip. But I don't do anything about moving. He does have nice aftershave on. Wonder what it is... There's no sign of Caitlin. Where did she go? Actually, come to think of it, I do remember her saying something about having a headache. Shit. She's gonna miss all the fun.

I'm not sure what happens next, but when I open my eyes again half the room is filled with the biggest rucksack I have *ever* seen. Bruce is there. He appears to be laughing and jumping up and down like I was when Sarah arrived. Somebody moves out of my line of vision and I'm remembering something about aeroplanes and someone called Byron.

The guy who Bruce is thumping on the back is wearing one of those T-shirts that were big in the eighties. Or was it the early nineties? Anyway, those T-shirts which change colour with body heat. This one is bright pink but the area around the shoulders and the armpits is purple. He's also wearing a pair of excruciatingly tight black jeans. Where did he come from? The Outback? Then I suddenly get a good look at his face. And oh my God, it is a *good* face. Brad Pitt meets Harrison Ford with a touch of Ewan MacGregor thrown in for good measure. Sarah appears at my side as if from nowhere and asks the guy with the teeth to go and get her a drink. She collapses in his vacated seat and says in a weird voice, 'Who is that guy, Kelly? Jesus, look at him. Why were you asking me to bring you sexy men? There isn't a man in *London* as sexy as that one.'

She's right, you know. This Byron, no, *Tyrone* man is incredible. Absolutely un-fucking-believable. I've got to meet him but I'm not sure if I can get to my feet. I don't have to. Before I know it, my wonderful, adorable flatmate is leading him towards me. Luckily Neil, or Ben or whoever he is, comes back at that moment and distracts Sarah. I might be drunk but the instinct is still strong. Survival of the fittest and all that.

The guy who must be Tyrone pulls me up to face level and gives me a big hug. I can see Bruce grinning. 'G'day Kelly. Good to meet ya. Heard a lot about you. Cheers for letting me stay for a bit.' I just smile inanely and can't believe that I'm too drunk to think straight. But hang on a second. Wait a minute. Hold it right there. He's Bruce's friend. *Bruce's*. That means that I can fancy him all I like and it won't make a damn bit of difference. This thought is a sobering one. I've never been in this situation before. Well, maybe the time I had a major crush on the school choir leader, but that was different. I didn't even know the *meaning* of the word homosexual then.

A minute later the rucksack, Bruce and Tyrone have gone, leaving a lot of open space in the middle of the lounge. A wilderness. I don't know what to do, but follow my gut feeling and move unsteadily in the direction of Bruce's room.

*

Bruce has put Tyrone's bag beside his cupboard and is putting a towel for him on the spare bed. He *is* going to sleep on the spare bed. Or is that just a ruse so as not to arouse Bill's suspicions? My thoughts are getting tangled and I stop in Bruce's doorway. I just stand there, propped up nicely by the doorframe. They don't even notice me they're so busy exchanging news of the last two years condensed into the two-minute version. I suddenly have a good idea and go to the kitchen. I'm back thirty seconds later with a whole tray of Sex on the Beach. I dumbly offer one to Tyrone and then manage something very unoriginal like 'Come on, you've got a lot of catching up to do.' He picks up the glass nearest to him and says that he's glad to see his old mate Bruce still knows how to party. The drink's gone in two seconds. 'Beer's my normal thing, but I'm in England. Time I tried something new.' Another glass is quickly emptied.

Bruce grabs one and downs his too. That's good. The more drunk they get the less obvious it will be how drunk I am. Bill appears in the door and puts his arm proprietarily around Bruce's waist. There's no reaction from Tyrone. I'm suddenly inspired and decide to take him on a guided tour of the flat. He's happy to comply.

I start off with my room, for some bizarre reason. The bed is piled high with coats. Tyrone and I make some crappy small talk about how he met Bruce and then move on to the exciting subject of jetlag. I know that I probably look really obvious because I'm drunk and therefore not shielding my real feelings, but I can't take my eyes off this man. I can't hold it in any longer. I've got to ask. 'So, how long did you and Bruce go out for? Was it a long-term thing?'

Tyrone looks puzzled, and then it's as if a big cartoon light bulb goes on above his head. 'I'm not *queer*. Is that what you thought? Hell, no. Me and Brucie have been mates since school. That's *all*.' I'm mentally criticising his use of the politically incorrect term when the meaning of what he's just said sinks in. I don't mean to say it, but I can't help it. It just slips out. 'It's my birthday today. Do you want to come to my party?' He looks at me in this mildly amused way, and says, 'I think I'm already at your party.'

He leans over, pushes me down on top of the coats and starts kissing me like I've never been kissed before. Australian men move fast. I like it. Please can this never end? The gods must be smiling down on me because it doesn't stop, not even when people come in and try to pull their coats out from under us. We just move to the spare bed in Bruce's room. I think at some point the door opens and Bruce and Bill come in, but they go away again. I fall asleep a few hours later with my arms around Tyrone's comfortable chest, my hands making purple marks on his T-shirt.

CHAPTER TWENTY-ONE

What day is it? Where am I? What happened? I wake up thinking that I should be hospitalised. Everything hurts. Oh my God! There's a man on the pillow. Highlights of last night begin to come back to me and my first coherent thought is that I have to emigrate. But where to? Australia's not far enough. My own bed would be a good start. I gently ease myself out from beneath the sleeping body. Tyrone. Bruce's friend. If I needed any further proof I get it in the form of the huge rucksack which I almost fall over as soon as I'm on my feet. Have to do a damage check. All my clothes are still in place, although my bra's undone. I can hear Bruce in my head saying, 'could have been a lot worse.' Oh God. What *is* Bruce going to say? I stole his best friend and held his room hostage. What are my friends going to say? Who was here last night anyway?

I'm halfway through the attempt to get back to my own room undetected when a hideously loud voice stops me in my tracks. Bruce. 'Hey sweetie! At least you're in your own house. I know how you hate doing that going home the next morning in last night's clothes thing.'

'I'm sorry, I'm sorry, I'm sorry. Please don't yell at me. Please don't hate me. You can have your friend back now. Wake me up in a month when he's gone. I'm very fragile today.' I force myself to look at Bruce. He's standing at the end of the hall with a white frilly apron tied round his waist and a pink feather duster in his hand. I have never seen him looking so camp. Five minutes ago I wouldn't even have thought laughter possible but now I can't help myself. I start giggling uncontrollably and slide down the wall until I'm sitting on the floor. Men are quite capable of giggling too and Bruce joins in and throws himself down beside me. He sticks the feather duster in my nose and I ineffectively start hitting him away. My stomach is aching and I'm out of breath. The laughter endorphins make me feel a lot happier and I suddenly have a desperate need to hear about everything I missed last night. I'm not yet ready to think about the reason I missed everything in the first place. Bruce puts on a Kenneth Williams voice: 'So, darling, did we achieve the desired combination of mellow music, sultry lighting and chic cocktails that you requested?'

It sounds like it was a great party. Paul and Caitlin left early on, cloak and dagger style. Probably couldn't contain themselves any longer. Sarah threw up in the bath. Lucy got Neil and Ben stoned and ended up snogging Neil. (Or Ben, Bruce isn't sure which.) Doug and Pete had a very public, very theatrical argument of epic proportions. Doug left in a huff and Pete spent the rest of the evening miming along to Boney M and Robbie Williams CDs. Declan and Jenny invited everyone to their wedding. They were talking about bringing the date forward because the dress will never fit if they wait until June. Bruce slept on my fold-down bed and Bill stayed on the couch. 'He's just popped out to buy some of that Stain Devils stuff. A jug of Black Russian got knocked over during a round of Twister.' (Damn, I'm sorry I missed the Twister.)

*

I scrub all of last night's make-up off and apply a fresh coat. I can't be bothered changing my clothes. I want a cigarette, a whole carton of orange juice, a coffee and a chat with Caitlin, in that order. My plan is disrupted halfway through the cigarette when Tyrone comes lumbering into the lounge. He actually lumbers. I grab the TV guide and try to look like I'm totally engrossed in it. He hasn't changed his clothes either, and those jeans look even worse in daylight. Yes, he may still be undeniably gorgeous but he has the most terrible dress sense *ever*. I don't know what to expect. I mean, I may have spent the night with him, but I don't know anything about him. Why, oh why has my heart started beating triple time? He probably lives on a farm in the bush, and refers to beers as *tinnies* and women as *sheilas*. Come on, *say* something.

'Geez, how can you smoke a cigarette this early in the morning?' That's *it*? That's the best he can come out with after I've just spent the whole night of my twenty-fifth birthday with him? I might have kidded myself that I didn't know what I was expecting but I did really. A kiss, a secret smile, a bunch of flowers maybe...

'It's not morning actually,' I retort defensively. 'It's twelve thirty in the afternoon.' He doesn't even reply. Just wanders over to where Bill is vigorously scrubbing the carpet and crouches down to inspect it and ask Bill what he's doing.

He doesn't mean anything to me. Nothing at all. He's just some Neanderthal who happened to be in the right place at the right time. I bet he doesn't even remember my name. I don't care. He's not my type anyway. Shit, but he's sexy.

I can't even call Caitlin because the phone's in the kitchen and there's too much risk of being overheard. (My mobile's permanently out of use until I pay the bill in full. I forgot that you don't have the option of just sending the minimum payment with a phone bill.)

The four of us spend the rest of the afternoon in a lethargic heap in front of the TV, only moving as far as the kitchen at sporadic intervals to get munchies. (Nobody ate the sushi. I certainly don't want it and it ends up in the bin.) I sit as far away from Tyrone as possible. It's one of those days when it feels like time is standing still. It's two o'clock for at least a couple of hours but then it's *suddenly* eight o'clock. When I go through to the kitchen to get a glass of orange juice Bruce follows me. He just wants to check if it's okay with me if he goes out for a drink with Bill and leaves

Tyrone here. 'He's too jetlagged to go anywhere, Kell. Better if he just gets the chance to veg out and get some rest.' I can't exactly demand that Bruce takes him to the pub and I certainly don't have the energy to go anywhere. I've got *work* tomorrow.

Just as Bruce and Bill are leaving, Caitlin phones. The first thing she says is 'Please don't hang up' which is a bit puzzling. She launches into this big apology spiel for being a bitch last night and tells me that she totally over-reacted and it was all because she was so scared of something going wrong between her and Paul. (It already has gone wrong, it's called a *wife*.) Anyway, as I don't remember her being a bitch, I decide to forgive her. She's so grateful. We can't speak long because she's about to go the gym (*the gym?*) so I tell her I have lots of news but we'll catch up properly in the week. Just before she rings off, she adds, 'Claudette is one of Paul's *colleagues*. Sarah met them at a pitch she put together at the advertising company where she works. I'm sorry again. I'm a stupid cow. Sorry. Speak to you soon.' Who's Claudette? I don't remember any Claudette being at the party. I must remember to ask Bruce in the morning.

*

I'm not going to be so childish as to go and sit in my room on my own. I'm also quite curious to see if Tyrone's capable of conversation. We watch *Heartbeat* in silence. I've switched over to the news before Tyrone actually says anything. 'Kelly,' (he does remember!) 'hope you don't think that last night didn't mean anything to me. Just didn't want to come on too strong in front of the others, you know. Thought you might be embarrassed or something. Friends?' Why on earth would I be embarrassed of this guy? He's perfect. At least now that he's said *that* he is. It would have been such an anticlimactic end to the weekend if I'd just ended up going to bed without having even discussed *us*.

'Course we're friends. Maybe a bit more than friends, right? You're going to be around for a while, so we may as well enjoy it.'

Bingo! He gets out of his seat and comes and sits beside me on the floor, in front of the log-effect electric fire. We'll have plenty of time to have conversations over the next month. For now, I'd be happy to see if he's as good a kisser as I (vaguely) remember him to be. He is. We miss the end of the news. We move to my bed. (Three coats are still on top of it for some reason and I push them onto the floor.) We succeed where we didn't succeed last night in getting each other's clothes off. We succeed in a lot more than that. It is the best sex I've ever had. (Not that I can really remember the best, so I decide this must be it.) Tyrone falls asleep really fast afterwards. Maybe it's the jetlag, but I'd prefer to think that I've worn him out. He's returned the favour. I'm knackered.

Just before I fall asleep (when I've almost finished analysing every single move we made) I hear Bruce coming in the front door. As soon as he goes into his room he'll see that Tyrone's not there. I hope he doesn't think I've lost him.

*

The alarm wakes me up after what feels like about six minutes. It's half past seven in the morning and I have to go to work. That's the bad thing about working for somebody you actually *like* – I can't not go. It doesn't look like anything will wake Tyrone. I try my best to make a lot of noise, banging the wardrobe door and stuff, but he doesn't move. I kind of wish he'd open his eyes and give me a goodbye kiss. Oh well, maybe he'll still be just where I left him when I get back from the play centre.

CHAPTER TWENTY-TWO

Over the last few days (my single life nothing but a distant memory) everything Australian, and therefore connected to Tyrone, has taken on a whole new significance. It's like when I was struggling to learn to drive. Every second car seemed to have L plates on. And on the rare yet unforgettable occasion I've had a pregnancy scare, I've bumped into pregnant women on every street corner. I mean, I just *opened* the newspaper today and five seconds later I'd discovered the Australian term 'pommie' derives from the words Prisoners of Her Majesty in Exile. In fact, 160,000 convicts were actually sent to Australia over a seven-year period. And I just *glanced* at the back of some guy's Financial Times on the way to work and saw that the Australian dollar has just hit a twelve-year low against the US dollar. Imagine that. A *twelve-year* low. *Crocodile Dundee* was on TV on Monday night (*again*). Last night I drank a glass of Jacob's Creek wine with dinner. When I went to the French patisserie for a cheese, bacon and avocado baguette at lunchtime, the girl who served me was...*Australian*! I bought some Aussie tea-tree oil spot cream in Boots yesterday – I just couldn't resist it. And the woman who sat beside me on the tube on my way home looked *exactly* like Madge from *Neighbours*. It's uncanny really.

Work's been fine. The party caused some female bonding thing to happen between me and Lucy. She keeps referring to it out of the blue in the middle of conversations. It's like 'Kelly, do you know where Karen's coat is? Oh! It was so funny when Doug actually started *crying*.' Or, 'Lauren's parents are late today. God! Neil thought I worked in *television*!' I always had a lot of respect for Lucy anyway, but now she's somehow more *normal*. I can really talk to her about things, although obviously not about stuff like the advantages of using Clinique products over an inferior brand such as Rimmel. I feel a bit bad that I didn't invite Doris and Wendy but I just don't think it would've been their scene. Last week Doris confided in me that she likes to listen to Daniel O'Donnell to help her unwind after a hard day, and Wendy spends most Friday and Saturday nights babysitting her sister's four children.

The last few days have taken their toll though. This morning there were only six kids on the boat. Sonia's in hospital getting some tests done, Cara's come down with this flu that everyone's getting and a couple of others were up all night and needed their sleep in the morning. We were all going a bit cabin crazy on The Laughing Duck so we decided to go for an impromptu trip to the park. It's been more years than I care to remember since I've run around after a ball. David thought I was just kidding around when I collapsed in a heap on the grass. When I got home I was too exhausted to jump into bed with Tyrone like I usually do. (We wait until the moment that Bruce gets on his bike in the afternoon and then dive under the covers.) Instead I did something that I've been looking forward to since Christmas. I've been saving a large, pink Bath Bomb that my grandmother gave me and which I couldn't bear to use until the right opportunity presented itself. It was a bit dusty but it still worked. You just drop it into the bath and it fizzles and dissolves in minutes, leaving rose petals floating all over the water. It would have been better if our bath was one of those huge free-standing Victorian ones with the clawed feet, but it was pretty good even in our olive-coloured plastic tub. Unfortunately it was broad daylight so I couldn't use candles to create a flattering light. I jumped in fast and reclined seductively in the pink water. By the time Tyrone had got his clothes off and turned round, all that was showing were my boobs, floating perkily on the surface.

He took the taps end and we scrubbed each other's backs so hard that I don't think I'll need to wash for a week. It was extremely invigorating, so much so that we managed to fit in a quickie before Bruce got back.

*

I meet Caitlin at six, in a crappy little bar that we particularly like. It's full of old men and fruit machines and lampshades with tassels on. We don't have to worry about who's just come in, or interrupt conversations to comment on so and so's Moschino shirt or whatever. We can just sit in a corner, buy countless diet cokes, and create an impenetrable fog of cigarette smoke around us. After bringing each other up to date on our love lives we have some serious issues on the agenda. We've concluded that we're both fantastically happy with our men (although I really must take Tyrone shopping on Oxford Street and give him some help in the fashion department). The issues in question are that Paul has a wife and Tyrone has a return ticket to Oz. Now that we've both got a guy in our lives at the same time, the possibilities for double dating are endless. Which is just one of the reasons that we don't like the threat of these relationships being anything other than long term. I mean, we're practically speaking favourite honeymoon destinations and babies' names here. Neither of us wants to be taken advantage of but neither of us is very good at playing hard to get, or laying down ultimatums. We've always believed in the same philosophy. Make them fall so hard in love with you that losing you is no longer a possibility. Just because this has never worked in the past, we see no reason why it won't work this time.

'I hate the feeling of things being temporary, Cait', I moan. 'Temporary work, temporary house, temporary diet, temporary hair-colour and now a temporary man. I want some damn security.'

'But if you play your cards right, Kell, one month just won't be long enough for him. He can probably extend his bloody ticket. But what about me? Remember, *''Til death do us part...'*

We do this a lot. We take turns complaining. We give the other our full attention, nod understandingly at all the right moments, throw in the odd sigh, wait for our go and then launch away. We may not accomplish much in this manner, or come to any actual conclusions, but it's remarkably therapeutic just to get all this stuff off your chest. Tonight is no exception. We both feel considerably more optimistic about our respective problems after discussing them in every possible light and speculating on every terrible outcome. Paul will walk into the office one day and make an announcement that his lovely wife, Marie-Claire, is expecting triplets. Tyrone will hate the English weather enough to drive him into bringing his departure date forward by two weeks. It feels so good to *share*!

*

Although I don't have half as much free time as I did, say, a month ago, I seem to be doing so much more. It's true what they say about you just having to *make* time. I've had to resort to Pro-Plus on a couple of occasions though. It's fine as long as I don't drink too many diet cokes shortly after taking them. If I do, it tends to result in trembling hands, weak legs and light-headedness. Or maybe that's just the effect Tyrone has on me. He really*is* good for me. And I think I'm good for him too. He doesn't seem to have thought about his photography since he got here. In fact, I haven't even noticed a camera among his possessions. I suspect that he just wanted to sound like he was doing something interesting when he wrote to Bruce. It's better this way though. He has so much free time to spend with me. I've promised to take him to see all the sights, including the Aquarium on the South Bank, which I've been dying to visit for ages. Up until now, however, we only seem to have moved between the bed and the pub. We've done a lot of talking though. I think he feels a bit unsure about his future, which is instantly something that we've got in common. He doesn't seem to have any concrete plans. He was doing some apprentice thing in a friend's construction company but decided that it wasn't really for him. I see him more as an architect. Or a designer. Obviously something creative, and preferably something using his hands. (He's very good with his hands.) And if we're going to have a future together, hopefully a job that makes a lot of money.

Not that we've talked about our future though. I know guys are usually slower to let their true feelings show. I don't want to push him. We've still got over three whole weeks to deal with that subject. Either he'll stay longer than he'd originally planned or I'll go out there. I've never been Down Under and I'd love to visit Ramsay Street. And see a koala bear. And learn how to surf. And learn to like beer. And stop washing my hair. In fact, it's probably a far better idea for me to go there. It'll be much easier for him to build a career in his own country, and I'll be able to pick up work anywhere. (Anywhere that's not London, that is.)

I've mentioned him to my mother, but just casually, in conversation. I didn't really let her know how serious we are. I know she'd probably start testing me on The Rules to make sure that I'd learned them all. I'm perfectly capable of running my own love life without the help of any stupid book. (And she's never thought much of Australians anyway. Says they lack class and culture.)

Bruce has rented *Priscilla, Queen of the Desert* for us to watch tonight. Bruce is really cool about me and Tyrone. I thought he might be a bit funny about it. I did worry that he'd be upset that Tyrone's spending more time with me than with him. I think it'd be worse if Bill wasn't in his life. It looks like things are getting a lot more serious between those two. So Bruce gets Tyrone in the morning, I get him in the afternoon and we can all spend time together in the evenings. It's perfect. He probably thinks Tyrone's a great boyfriend for me. You know, someone he's known for a long time and really trusts. I think Fluffy's feeling a bit left out, although I do always make a point of going to say hello to him as soon as I get home.

An invitation to Declan and Jenny's wedding arrived today. They've moved the date forward to April the 28th. That's the day before Tyrone's due to leave. Maybe I'll be so busy packing that I'll be too stressed to go to a wedding. Anyway, we've all accepted. Bruce is bringing Bill. The actual ceremony's going to be in a registry office, but they're having a big evening do in a hotel. In a village called Bramley, I think. I've never been to Surrey. It'll be nice to get out to the country. Weddings are always so emotional. Hopefully, it'll put some ideas into Tyrone's head.

CHAPTER TWENTY-THREE

I really wanted to go out to dinner in a romantic restaurant with Tyrone last night but he insisted on staying in and watching Australian rules football. I think he's probably feeling a bit guilty about coming all this way to visit his mate and then falling in love with his mate's *flatmate*. And then today, when I got home from work, Tyrone had borrowed a neighbour's bike and gone for a cycle with Bruce. That's *our* time. Anyway, it gave me the chance to shave my legs and pluck my eyebrows. And write birthday thank-yous, which normally take me about a month to get around to.

They get back after a couple of hours. Tyrone's looking deliciously sweaty. I'm expecting him to come and give me a big kiss but he just sits down on the couch and turns on the telly. I know it's probably difficult for him to hold himself back when Bruce's around, but I have *needs*.

Worse still, when I suggest us all going to a club tomorrow night (I have an urge to splash out on a sexy new outfit for the occasion) Bruce quickly tells me that they're having a lads' night out. What? Bruce has never been a lad. I suppose he thinks Tyrone's got certain expectations and that he has to make an effort. I'm going to have to make some plans with the girls immediately. I'm certainly not in the mood to spend another Saturday night alone, watching *Blind Date* and thinking about everyone else in the whole of London out partying. And it'll be good to make Tyrone wonder what I'm getting up to while he's drinking boring beer in a boring bar watching boring sports on satellite TV.

I offer to cook dinner but Bruce says they'd planned to get a Chinese. That's okay. I'll just go and file my nails until it arrives.

*

It's almost one in the morning and I'm sitting up in bed telling Tyrone about the whole Simply the Best thing. I play on his protective male instincts and make it sound a bit worse than it actually was; my top was ripped right off my body, Stelios' rough hand grabbed my breasts, Tomas continued filming the whole thing. My descriptions might not make him feel exactly protective, but he certainly gets horny. We have the best sex we've had since last Sunday. Everything's okay.

*

On Saturday, Bruce, Bill, Tyrone and I all buy one day travel passes and do London. Madame Tussauds, the Planetarium, the Tower of London, Buckingham Palace and the Aquarium. I hate queues. Why do so many people want to *come* here? Tyrone makes it all worthwhile though. He acts like the archetypal tourist and buys all the guidebooks and a couple of souvenir T-shirts. (I presume they're just keepsakes – he wouldn't honestly wear them out of doors, would he?) In the wax museum he patriotically lingers longest in front of Kylie Minogue. Complains that Danni should be there too. The Aquarium is really amazing but Bruce and Tyrone say that the sharks are just tiddlers compared to the ones they've seen in the ocean back home. (*Yeah, sure.*) Tyrone starts teasing that one of those really ugly fishes with the big mouths looks like me. I try to laugh, but I can't help taking stuff like that personally. It makes me paranoid. Does he really think my mouth's too big? Or is it just boys being boys? I have to decide on the latter or I won't get any peace of mind for the rest of the day.

We eat our evening meal in Burger King. I order a Whopper and Tyrone says that I'd better be careful or I'll get fat. Oh God. I bet he was really thinking fatt*er*. The thought weighs heavily on my mind and the burger's going to weigh heavily on my thighs. I can't even enjoy the food. What's wrong with me today? I do a quick mental calculation to see if it's PMT. It's not.

Unbelievably – because this never happens in London – we bump into Sarah and her friend Jane in the tube station on our way home. I've only met Jane once before. I think she's a lesbian. This is awful. Sarah is practically throwing herself at Tyrone. He looks happy to see her and gives her a hug, and says cutely, 'How're you going?' Personally, I wish she was going home. Immediately. She's giggling and twiddling her hair. She playfully tells him that she would have liked to have had the chance to speak to him at the party but that he disappeared too quickly. Says that she was stuck with her friend Ben, who she'd only brought along as a favour to me. The *bitch*! In those few words she's managed to imply that: (a) she's interested in Tyrone, (b) she has no problem finding available men to bring along to parties, and (c) I'm completely sad and desperate. Just wait until I speak to Caitlin about this. I'm practically dragging the boys in the opposite direction as I say airily, 'I'll call you when I find the time Sarah. Just been *sooo* busy lately.'

'Don't rush off, Kell. Since this is such a huge coincidence I think we should make the most of it and have a drink. There's a stunning cocktail bar just outside the station.' If looks could kill Sarah would be on the ground by now, and people would just be stepping over and around her, thinking that she's crazy, drunk, or both.

'Sorry, Sarah. We've got to get ready to go out. It *is* Saturday night so we are actually in a bit of a rush.' As I say this I realise that I didn't remember to make any girlie plans for tonight so I don't, in fact, have anything to get ready for. Caitlin's seeing Paul and I *had* planned on calling

Sarah. Obviously I won't be doing any such thing after *this*. I'll have to go out on my own. I just *cannot* be at home, sitting on the sofa in my pyjamas when the guys are out having fun.

'I'm up for a bevvy. All this sightseeing has been bloody hard work.' Tyrone heads for the *up* escalator, and the rest of us have no option but to follow. Not that that's a problem for Sarah. She's like a damn puppy. Bruce looks at me with a sympathetic expression. He's very sensitive and can spot a bitch a mile away. How have I never noticed this side to Sarah before? Probably it's because we've never been in a situation before where we've both been attracted to the same man. She likes *black* men, for God's sake. Couldn't she tell that me and Tyrone are together? I mean, we weren't holding hands or anything because he told me that he isn't comfortable with public displays of affection, but she could have guessed. He *did* keep checking behind him that I was still following.

The bar is gorgeous, and all the people who are in it are gorgeous too. I'm wearing a comparatively horrible outfit which is *so* last year. Everyone thinks the place is wonderful and I am so pissed off that I didn't find it and introduce everyone to it. We sit around a big, circular, stainless steel table and I'm stuck beside Jane. She starts talking about something but I can't really concentrate because I'm trying to eavesdrop on everyone else's conversations. As a result, I must look like a right bimbo to Jane, and this gives me one more thing to be paranoid about. I'm horrified when I hear mention of the guys meeting up with Sarah and her friends later tonight. She knows all the right places. Says she can get them in for free. Has a friend who'll make sure their names are 'on the list'. I am stuck behind Jane and am totally excluded from this conversation. I'm desperate to get out of here but it must be at least an hour until everyone starts to make a move. Our drinks are ridiculously expensive and I hate Sarah for having a real job. Not only that, but a real job that she loves. And a tiny bum. And fantastic *naturally* arched eyebrows. She doesn't wake up with them smudged halfway across her forehead like I do. I'm still at the stage of making sure that I'm always out of bed and in the bathroom for a touch-up before Tyrone sees me.

We finally get on the bloody train and thankfully it's going in the opposite direction to Sarah. I don't say anything all the way home. I'm waiting for someone to ask me what's wrong so I can just say 'nothing' and dramatically brush a single tear from my eye, but nobody does.

When we get home Tyrone runs around the flat looking for a clean pair of jeans (he's lived in those black ones all week) and Bruce goes to do his hair. I am utterly dejected. I know I'm not included because they're still acting on the pretence that it's a boys' night out, but I absolutely know that Sarah will somehow just bump into them later. Another amazing *coincidence*.

I go and sit outside on the front step and have a cigarette. It's bloody freezing and I want Tyrone to come out, put his arms around me and say that he's changed his mind. That he really wants to have a quiet night. Just the two of us (and a can of whipped cream). The only company I get though is next door's cat. He comes and pushes his head against my arms and tries to climb onto my lap. This only makes me more miserable. I don't even have a cat to love me. Fluffy does his best, but it's not like he can sleep in my bed or anything. I have to go back inside before I get a chill. I kiss the cat goodbye.

*

It's about midnight. Probably a couple of hours until the guys get home. I did have a plan of getting all dressed up and walking around the block at about the time they were due home. Turning up ten minutes after them and telling them that I had an absolutely incredibly good night. But the time scale is too dodgy. I'd probably get raped hanging around the streets in a short skirt and heels. Instead, I'm just embarking on my second tub of Häagen-Dazs (the large size). This one's cookies 'n' cream flavour which is good, but not as good as the pralines 'n' cream one that

I've already finished. I will at least have to hide the evidence before the others get home. It would just look so terrible if they came in and found me asleep on the couch surrounded by empty ice-cream cartons.

When the last spoonful's finished I feel really sleepy. There's a half-decent Michael Douglas thriller on which I've been following and I really want to see what happens in the end. But I'm tired. I'll just lie down and close my eyes and listen to what they're saying. God, the volume's a bit high. Keeps making me jump when a noisy bit comes on. I'll just turn it down a bit. Shit. Just. Can't. Stay. Awake...

CHAPTER TWENTY-FOUR

I'm woken up in the early hours of the morning by Tyrone jumping on top of me, which is a relief, because for a minute I thought I was in the middle of another earthquake. In fact, as I wake up fully, I remember that I was more than a little worried he'd be jumping on top of someone else tonight. But he's come home to *me*. I don't think he's even noticed the evidence of my little binge. I lean over and surreptitiously shove the cartons and the spoon under the sofa.

'Hey babe. Bruce's gone back to Bill's place so we're all alone.' His breath smells like a brewery and his skin's all scratchy because he hasn't shaved for a couple of days. I throw my arms around his neck regardless. He lifts me up and carries me through to my room. (He's a little unsteady but I'm sure that's just because he's had one beer too many.) He *lifts me up*! I've always wanted a strong man for that very reason. I wiggle my toes in the air, make squealing noises, and pretend that I want him to put me down. He doesn't do so until I'm hovering directly over the bed, and then we fall onto it together.

Tyrone may not be very good in the finesse department, but he makes up for it in the trouser department. I do wish he'd spend a bit more time kissing and cuddling first. Or stroking my back in just the right place. I'd be far too embarrassed to mention it though. Anyway, I fall asleep happy, the evening's misery forgotten. Damn, I missed the end of that thriller. I'll never know what happens at the end. That's the second time I've seen it and I didn't make it to the end the other time either.

*

I attempt to make a full roast lunch on Sunday. Bruce and Bill are back. Bill's a veggie but he's not difficult about it and said that he wouldn't mind just having all the trimmings without the meat. I remembered a can of spaghetti hoops in the cupboard which at least brightened up his plate a bit. Unfortunately, I think he probably enjoyed the spaghetti hoops more than the rest of us enjoyed the beef. It was horrible. All chewy and flavourless. I think I might become a vegetarian too. It would certainly be a good reason to never have to cook roast beef again. Even the potatoes didn't taste right. I should have phoned my mother for some advice but I just couldn't bring myself to. She would have gone on for hours anyway and bored me stupid, and she wouldn't have approved of the fact I was using the microwave instead of the oven. (Well there was no way I was going to get up at six in the morning to start defrosting.)

I love the idea of going for a long walk in the park after lunch but my body doesn't agree. I get comfy on the sofa and do the crossword from yesterday's paper. When I'm at the last clue (*Female spouse – four letters*) the phone rings. The boys are all in Bruce's room, busy getting brainwashed by a computer programme so I have to force myself to get up and answer it. It's Sarah. I'm so glad I answered the call because I can lie, and say that we're all about to go out for a drink and that no, it's not okay for her to pop round and borrow my copy of *Feel the Fear and Do It Anyway*. What a see-through bloody story. She may as well have asked to come all the way across London to borrow a cup of sugar. I'm certainly not going to lend her any damn self-help book. *Or* my boyfriend, for that matter. Bruce told me that they never got round to going to the club that Sarah said she'd see them in last night. They actually ended up staying in the one bar all night because it had a pool table. Sarah must be worried that her pulling powers are failing. Thank God Bruce didn't answer the phone. He would have told her that we weren't going anywhere and that it'd be okay for her to come over. I'm just going to have to be vigilant and try and answer the phone every time it rings.

My mother phones a couple of hours later, and I wish I hadn't made that stupid rule about answering the phone. I don't really want to hear all about the super dinner party my parents went to at the Robbs' house last night. 'And their daughter Meg is doing exceptionally well at the BBC. The chances are good that she'll be promoted to Continuity Announcer within the next six months.' Goddamn it. I hold my chin up high and tell my mother about the simply delicious roast I cooked for lunch.

I absolutely can't avoid going to the launderette any longer and bravely decide to head to the new place down the road that's open seven days a week. Bruce hand-washes, and never seems to amass the mountains of crusty clothes that I do. Three black bin bags full today. This is one of the chores that I really have to grit my teeth to get through. I'd never even been inside a launderette until I came to London (the cosy, sociable laundry room in university halls doesn't count). Whenever I walk in I feel like I'm entering the set of *Eastenders*. I invariably forget to bring the huge bottle of two-in-one washing liquid/fabric conditioner from the kitchen and have to fork out a couple of extra quid for the mini-size portions of it in the vending machine. Today is no exception. But I did remember to bring The Stage to read. I never knew washing machines *took* so long until I had to sit in front of one waiting impatiently for it to finish.

It's only when I'm all sorted out and have got the Daz out of the machine that I realise there aren't actually any washing machines free. There aren't many people around but they must have all left their clothes spinning and are going to come back for them later. I'm about to sit down and wait when a guy appears in front of me. He's the one who got his hands on the last available machine. He's an ageing hippie with greying hair and a worn-looking face. He smells of whisky. I hate those situations when a total stranger starts asking questions: 'What's your name? Where do you come from? What do you do?' I never know what to say. I totally don't want to share any details of my life with this weirdo but I don't want to look like a pathetic idiot refusing to even tell him my name. It's a no-win situation. He susses out my problem regarding the obvious lack of washing machines. He tells me that he's just got back from a month in Thailand and points out the huge, multicoloured heap of filthy clothes on the shelf above the machines. He tells me that I should put my coloureds in with his and we can split the one pound eighty. I look over at the bedraggled heap of stuff and almost puke at the thought of putting my delicate black lace undies in with that. I tell him that I've just remembered something I've urgently got to do and make a sharp exit. He calls after me that he's got a car and can give me a lift anywhere I want to go. I ignore him. I hate that. Now I can't even wait for a machine because I know I'd be hassled and I just can't be bothered. I'm going to have to wear my horriblest, baggy knickers until I next work up the energy to go to the launderette. I think I might look into how much it costs to rent a washing machine. I'm sure it'd be worth it.

When I get home I tell the boys all about the gorgeous guy who just spent ages chatting me up in the laundrette. I said he looked like the one in that Levi's ad, but that he didn't take his jeans off so I didn't hang around. I'm convinced that Tyrone is unusually attentive for the rest of the evening. He won't be when he sees the underwear I've got on.

*

Doris is off work on Monday and Tuesday with the flu. She probably caught it off Cara last week. It makes a big difference being one down – I don't know how Lucy managed in the mornings before I came along. Maybe I should warn her about the imminent possibility of me emigrating to Australia. She might want to start advertising for someone. I think I'll leave it until I've gone over it with Tyrone. Usually Doris stays on in the afternoon to help Lucy. Wendy's got classes in the afternoon and can't make it so I offer to do it until Doris is back. It's so much harder working a full day. There are only about three or four kids in the afternoon, but Lucy's organised an individual syllabus for each of them to follow and we have to make sure they're keeping up. There's a thirteen-year-old boy called Jack, who's blind. All his books are in Braille. I'd never actually seen a Braille book before and I'm fascinated. I should be quizzing him about what he's just read but I spend all the time asking him about how he learnt Braille instead. He seems to like the break from his studies and tells me that he even gets comics in Braille. The afternoon session finishes at six, and technically I can leave then but I feel obliged to stay and help Lucy with the cleaning up. I don't get home until about seven thirty. It's terrible. Getting up, going to work, coming home, watching TV, going to bed and then it all starts again the next day. I can't even find the time to phone Caitlin or paint my toenails.

Thankfully Doris is back on Wednesday. Still a bit sniffly but over the worst of it. I go home and spend a lazy afternoon watching chat shows with Tyrone. There's one about women who marry gay men just for the security and companionship it offers, even though they *know* they're gay. I might have considered that before Tyrone came along. I mean, Bruce is a great flatmate. He's got a good job. And a bike. And my parents would be happy for *anyone* to take me off their hands.

*

The phone call comes at nine fifteen. Doris is dead. Lucy is sobbing down the phone, telling me that it was a massive heart attack and that nothing could be done. Frank, her husband, phoned Lucy as soon as the doctor had been. Said Doris had just finished washing the dishes and was sitting down with her new copy of Woman's Realm when it happened. Lucy's already phoned round all the parents and closed the play centre for the rest of the week. Says it would just be too emotional going in. Doris has been there with her right from the very beginning. She's been a rock to Lucy, providing support and advice whenever it was asked for. The thought flashes across my mind that I won't have to go to work for the next couple of days which is good at least. How could I think that? It just hasn't sunk in yet. I don't really believe that I won't be going to The Laughing Duck tomorrow morning like usual, and Doris will be there, a smile on her face and a child hanging onto each hand. I think it really makes you aware of your own mortality when someone around you dies. I mean, I spend so much time wishing the days away. You know, can't wait until lunchtime, can't wait until the weekend, can't wait until I can retire and spend all day drinking gin and eating cream cakes. Not that Doris did that though. She always put everybody else before herself. I can't imagine what her husband must be going through tonight. And her children. She has two sons, not much older than me.

Bruce and Tyrone try their best to say the right things, and Bruce goes and makes me a cup of tea. But they never even *met* Doris. I go to bed early and the tears hit me. I keep remembering how nice Doris was to me on my first day on the boat. She even shared her scone with me at snack-time. I'm still crying long after Tyrone's come through to bed and fallen asleep.

CHAPTER TWENTY-FIVE

The funeral is on Saturday. It doesn't feel like a Saturday though. It feels like a bleak, miserable Monday. I bought a new long black skirt for it. It felt really weird going into a shop and buying something for the specific purpose of wearing it to a funeral. It just didn't feel *right*, all that teen-pop music and the bright colours and there was me, trying on this skirt, checking in the mirror to make sure it didn't make my bum look too big.

Lucy's parents have come down from Yorkshire to offer some support. She's taken it very badly, but I'm not surprised. You can't blame her. Doris was like a second mother to her. I get a taxi and meet Lucy and her family at the church. It's drizzling lightly and her dad's carrying the biggest umbrella I've ever seen. Everyone's finding it difficult to smile. I pass Lucy a note that I wrote for her. It wasn't easy to find the right words but I wanted to let her know that I understand how much Doris meant to her and that she can speak to me whenever she needs to (not that my advice would be anything like as good as Doris's). Frank is standing near the door to the church. Kind of hovering outside like he doesn't want to go in. He's managing to shake people's hands, receive their words of sympathy and make a suitable response to each. I don't know how he can do it. His heart must be in a thousand pieces.

I never feel comfortable in church at the best of times. I get this panicky feeling that there's no hope in me suddenly turning to God and asking for His help just beçause the surroundings inspire it. The only funeral I've been to before was that of an elderly aunt. I was too young to really understand what was going on. I couldn't appreciate the solemnity of the occasion and screamed and kicked when my mother wouldn't let me take my Sindy doll into the church. But I have no problem understanding the solemnity of today. Those must be Doris's and Frank's sons. They're both tall. One of them has a beard. They move towards their father and the three of them move into the church vestibule. We all follow.

It sounds strange to say the service was 'good' but I definitely think that the minister summed up Doris and spoke eloquently of how greatly she'll be missed. She was a member of the congregation in this church for the last twenty years and was well known and loved in the parish. The thought crosses my mind that if I were to die tomorrow I would have made no mark on society, made no gesture of charity or selflessness. I start to get paranoid and everything begins to feel very surreal. We sing 'Onward Christian Soldiers' at the end but I keep losing my place in the hymn book because my eyes are blurry. Oh God. What are we going to tell the children on Monday? Maybe their parents will have already explained it to them. Maybe we could hold some kind of memorial service. Plant a tree in her memory or something.

The burial takes place in the graveyard round the back of the church. The rain is getting harder which seems fitting. My heels are sinking into the mud so I have to try to walk on tiptoe. I know it's a very trivial thing to consider at a time like this, but it's impossible to ignore. When the minister has finished, and the coffin has been lowered, Frank throws a single white rose down after it. At least the rain camouflages our tears.

I say a few quick but heartfelt words to Frank afterwards. I politely decline the invitation to go on to his house for tea and sandwiches. I think it would be too much for me to be in a place where Doris's presence and influence could be so strongly felt. Her charity collection boxes and

Daniel O'Donnell tapes are just where she left them. I just know I'd be overcome with sympathy for her family. I say goodbye to Lucy and her parents who are going with Frank. Lucy and I hug tightly and I say I'll phone her tomorrow.

I don't feel like going back to the flat straight away. Somehow I need to linger on my own in the rain, and let my head sort itself out. I have this sense of something being very wrong in my life. Maybe it's just the feeling of injustice over Doris's premature death. I walk along the canal and little things are so poignant. The homeless man in his sleeping bag underneath the bridge. The graffiti on the walls. The rubbish floating on the water. It's a black day.

*

The weekend feels long and sad. Bruce and Tyrone went out on Saturday night but I just wanted to stay at home, have a hot bath and read a book. When Tyrone got back and got into bed I couldn't believe it when he tried to wake me up, his hands all over me. I didn't want to get upset all over again so I just pretended to be asleep. He can be very insensitive sometimes, but then, aren't all men?

I spoke to Lucy on Sunday afternoon. She's sounding a bit stronger and says that she has to go back to the boat tomorrow. If she leaves it any longer it will only be harder. I don't want to upset her more, but I ask what she's planning to do about the afternoons. I'd offer to go if she was stuck, but I wouldn't choose to be there all day given the option. The children are very demanding, and although I'm beginning to really care about them, it would wear me out to be there all day, every day. It isn't an issue though because Wendy has rearranged some classes, asked to borrow notes from friends and phoned Lucy to say she'll do afternoons for as long as necessary. Wendy's a good person. I think she'll make an excellent nurse one day. All I can say is, rather her than me. Those *shoes*.

On Sunday night I venture out to the local pub with Tyrone, Caitlin and Bruce. It's pretty quiet, just a few old men propping up the bar and a couple of students. It's very relaxing. I love being surrounded by these three. Bruce is bitching about how uncomfortable the seat of his bike is after riding for anything longer than twenty minutes. Caitlin says it's because his bum is too bony, and I tell him about a gel-filled bike seat I saw in a catalogue. I must try and find the page for him when we get home. Bruce picks up a discarded Mail on Sunday from a nearby table and reads out everyone's horoscopes. Mine says *Conflicts and problems at home, at work and in relationships come to a head this week. Don't get angry and complicate matters. Enlist the support of friends and work out your winning strategy.* Great. Caitlin's says something about Venus smiling on her and how the focus is purely on love. Why couldn't mine be like that? I don't know how I can be expected to come up with a winning strategy for *my* life within a week. I really must discuss things with Tyrone though. He's only here for another fortnight and I know it's going to pass quickly. I feel like I'm in limbo. I'm impatient and I want to know what's happening. There's no point applying for more jobs here if I'm going to move away. I'm glad that I met Lucy, and I think I've learnt a lot on the boat. But for Lucy, the play centre is her purpose in life. She's believed in it and worked towards it for as long as she can remember. I'm just the paid help. I need to find my own thing.

I haven't eaten much all weekend and when I get home I'm starving. I eat three packets of crisps, a pot noodle, two apples and half a packet of chocolate Hob-Nobs. I feel much better. Bruce rubs my shoulders and I almost fall asleep on the sofa. I let Fluffy out for a runabout and he's delighted. He tries to climb up the curtains but keeps slipping down, his little claws making scratchy noises. He looks so funny that I go and get my camera and take a few pictures. Then Bruce takes a picture of me and Tyrone and I take one of Tyrone and Bruce. I can't wait to see them when they're developed.

When I go through to bed I can't stop thinking about what it's going to be like tomorrow at the play centre. I've just taken off the last shred of clothing (I'll soon have run out of even the most horrible of my last resort underwear) when Tyrone bursts through the door and takes a picture of me. I go mental. I scream and shout and tell him that he can sleep on the fold-down bed. I'm not in the mood for company. I want to be able to stretch out and have the bed all to myself. This must be the first 'conflict in a relationship' the bloody horoscope mentioned. But shit, what was he thinking? Now I'll be too embarrassed to get the photos developed at Boots like usual. I'll have to find one of those companies where you send your film away in an envelope and they develop it and send it back. I think it's quite a bargain actually. But that's not the point. I always get my pictures done in the one-hour service because I'm so impatient to see them.

Tyrone looks like a kid who's been shouted at. I end up feeling bad for blowing up and join him on the fold-down bed. We have fast and furious sex. It is a good way of releasing tension. When we're done, Tyrone looks me in the eyes and says, 'I really like you, Kell.' Well, that's *something*.

*

Monday isn't quite as bad as expected. Lucy said a few words about how Doris was old and that she's gone to heaven. That she's watching all of us from up there. Some of the kids understood but others looked vacant. David piped up that his goldfish is in heaven but that it's okay because he got a rabbit instead. This is a real icebreaker and Lucy visibly relaxes, gives herself a mental shake, and starts getting the crayons and paper ready. We're going to draw wild animals. It's time we had some new decorations on the windows. Spring is almost here.

CHAPTER TWENTY-SIX

A letter arrives for me on Tuesday from that Middle East Broadcasting company that I applied to ages ago. It's not actually a straight rejection for once. The letter is quite friendly really, and explains that the position they advertised has already been filled. However, there's a junior position as a runner and researcher in Tel Aviv that they feel I might be qualified for. It's probably just a nice way of saying 'no thanks' but I type out a second application after work and stick it in the post. I'm not exactly going to be holding my breath. I'd almost forgotten about that one anyway and the chances are I'll be starting a new life Down Under.

Lucy comes round for a meal when she's finished on the boat. She's still feeling a bit low and we're going to have a *Friends* evening. The plan is to watch the whole of series three. I make my pasta dish because I know that nothing can go wrong. Everyone likes it and Bruce says it's even better than the one I made the night my parents came over. (My new Magic Garden is growing nicely on top of the wardrobe in my bedroom.) Tyrone eats more than anyone else and I'm more than a little pleased about that. Especially since the only time he's tasted my cooking before, it was an absolute disaster. Lucy offers to help clean up afterwards but I send her through to the lounge and tell her to skin up. She said that she's got some excellent grass and I'm in the mood for a smoke.

Four hours of *Friends* later, we're all completely wasted and Lucy and I moan about having to get up in the morning. She gets a cab because the last tube went at half past twelve. Tyrone and I go through to my room and just as he's pulling off my socks, I'm inspired to have the big conversation I've been practising in my head practically since the first moment I met him.

'Tyrone, it's less than two weeks until your flight home. Will you miss London?' I think it's better to ease into this gently.

'Not the weather for sure, but I'll miss *you*, sweetheart. You should feel what summer's like in Oz. You wouldn't believe it.' See! He does want me to go to Australia. He couldn't have put it much blunter than that. I'm momentarily distracted by thoughts of which brand of suntan cream I'll buy.

'Course it's almost gonna be winter by the time I get back but it's nothing compared to an English one. You don't get snow where I come from.'

That's thrown me. I presumed Tyrone was inviting me to spend a lazy, hazy summer with him but it's not going to *be* summer. And he said he'd miss me. He can't miss me if I'm with him, cooking him good food and ravaging his body the moment he gets home from work. I have to push at this a bit more.

I go for the light, casual approach though. I don't want him to notice that this is a serious conversation. Going on past experience, men don't like that kind of thing. 'Well maybe you should pack me in your suitcase. As soon as you open it we'll go for a run on the beach and end up tangled up in the surf having the best sex ever. Like in that old classic black and white film. What's it called? *From Here to Eternity*, I think.' He looks blank. 'We can cook breakfast together and you can show me the sights.'

'Dunno what my oldies would think of that, Kell. They're a bit conservative, if you know what I mean.'

I don't understand the relevance. 'What would your folks have to do with it, sexy? We could go and visit them and be on our best behaviour.'

'What do you mean, *visit* them? I still *live* with them. You know, not having a steady wage and all that.'

Oh my God. He still lives with his *parents*. All my visions of us naked on top of his kitchen table disappear pretty damn fast. I can't believe this. He never told me that before, but I suppose I just presumed he had his own place, or at the very worst, shared with mates. I never even *asked*. Shit. I don't quite know how to continue with this now. I thought he'd be able to *look after* me. I get straight to the point. 'I'd been hoping that I could come out, you know, be with you. I don't know what I'll do when you've gone. I don't like the weather here much myself. Or you could stay longer. It's no problem for us, you're a great guest to have around.' I pinch his bum as I say that last bit.

He looks slightly awkward for a moment, but then his frown disappears. 'Tell you what, as soon as I'm home I'll look into getting a place of my own. Or even sharing with my mate Kenny. I'm pretty sure he's got a spare room and he could do with a bit of money. It might be a laugh, you know. My mysterious British girlfriend arriving just days after I get back. My mates would be bloody impressed.'

His mates being impressed is not the reason for him wanting me there that I'd hoped for, but it'll do. Mission accomplished. It'll be better this way because I can spend the few days between him going and me joining him to get organised and pack my stuff.

Feeling that a great weight's been lifted off my shoulders, I climb on top of him and start to show him why he can't possibly live without me.

*

I have a wonderful lunch after work on Wednesday with Caitlin. She's suitably impressed by my news. Makes a big fuss about how much she's going to miss me and not having anyone to talk to about Paul. Their affair is still very hush-hush. No mention of him leaving his wife yet. We discuss strategies over our ciabatta sandwiches. I think Caitlin should make him jealous and go out with other people now and then. Or if that's not as easy as it sounds, at least make Paul *think* that she's seeing other people. But that's just too much of a risk for Caitlin. She could be right. I bet there's loads of other women he comes into contact with every day and who would be quite happy to fill Caitlin's shoes. It's not a very loyal thought to Cait, but if he's done it once you can never be sure that he's not going to do it again. Look at Will Carling.

Caitlin doesn't have much on this afternoon, so she manages to fit in a couple of hours wandering down Oxford Street with me. I know I should be saving every penny towards my flight but I see a shirt that I can't resist getting for Tyrone. And a beach towel in John Lewis that I buy for myself. And a few bottles of Hawaiian Tropic suntan oil. I can't wait until I have a tan again.

Then something awful happens. It's made all the more awful because I'm on my own. Caitlin's finally headed back to her desk. I'm just crossing the road opposite Benetton to go to the underground when it happens. Somehow, my heel gets caught on a rough bit on the road and completely tears off. Well, it doesn't actually *fall* off. It's just dangling like a wobbly tooth. I can't walk on it, and I'm not going to hop. I can't stand in the middle of the road either. I manage to make it to the safety of the other side by way of a kind of slow shuffle. I look around me to see if anyone's noticed. Two teenage girls in white Puffa jackets have. They're giggling and pointing. They're too far away for me to hear them but I can just imagine what they're saying. You know, 'Look at that stupid cow in the high heels. *Imagine* that happening to you. She'll have to go home in bare feet.' I will certainly not go home in bare feet. God knows what I'd be stepping on. But I know I can't navigate the stairs down to the station like this. I feel like crying. As the two girls walk past me the fatter of them says snidely, 'Enjoy your trip?' They're still laughing as they walk off. Stupid bitches. I'd rather lose a heel than wear the Kickers they've both got on. Why do things like this always happen to me? The big branch of Top Shop is just across the road and I know it sells Faith shoes. I'm sure I've got their store card somewhere in my purse.

It might only be across the road but I feel like I'm crossing the Antarctic. In the end, I yank off the offending heel and walk safely, if a bit lopsidedly, across the road. I am *so* self-conscious as I go down the escalator. I must look like a bag lady. In the shoe department I don't see anything that immediately leaps out at me, but this is no time for comparison shopping. I try not to think of the stunning pair of shoes I saw in Russell & Bromley's last week. This is a total *waste* of shoe-shopping. I have no choice but to find something here. I try on a pair of black platforms with ankle straps but they're too small. In growing desperation I ask for a pair of black mules in a size six. These ones fit and I say that I'll keep them on and ask the guy to put my old ones in a bag. I can't meet his eye as I say it. I am absolutely *mortified*. There's no way I'm going to tell anyone about this. Except Caitlin of course. If only she hadn't left when she did. It wouldn't have been half as bad if I could've leaned on her shoulder and laughed all the way to Russell & Bromley's. It's always worse when you embarrass yourself in public and you're on your own. You look ten times more pathetic. I still remember the time when I was still at school and walked right past the nearby boy's school on my way home with my skirt tucked into my knickers.

The shoes set me back £44.95. I bloody hope I like them enough to wear them again. Maybe I should start carrying around a spare pair in case of emergencies. But there's already enough junk in my handbag as it is.

As I'm waiting on the platform for my train I'm convinced I see Stelios. I panic and break into a sweat. I find a pair of shades that are still in my bag from last summer and put them on. Maybe the other people around will mistake me for a celebrity. I stand there shaking for at least two minutes until I realise that it's not him. Same hair and eyes but this guy's too short. And Stelios had better dress sense. And this guy's pushing a pram. I really think it's time I left this city. Too many bad memories. Too many people full stop. I daydream about barbecues and bareback horseriding along the beach, wearing only a pair of denim cut-offs and a white halter neck top, until the train comes.

CHAPTER TWENTY-SEVEN

On Friday night Tyrone and Bill go to see an old Bruce Lee film that's showing at the Prince Charles. It doesn't appeal to me or Bruce. It's the first time in ages that we've actually spent time together without anyone else around. He seems a bit concerned about my forthcoming move to Australia. I've just shown him the working visa I got today from the Australian embassy. It's valid for twelve months.

'Don't you think this is a bit drastic, Kell? I mean, Tyrone's a great guy but you're just beginning to do okay here. You've got the boat and you're still applying for other stuff. The right job's bound to turn up sooner or later. It's a long way to go. What do your parents think about it?'

I haven't actually told my parents yet. I *will*, it's just that I've been very busy. I think I should just say that Tyrone and I are friends. And there *are* a lot of job opportunities out there. They can come and visit me. They've never been further than Florida.

'No problem, Bruce. They won't worry about me so much when there's that much distance between us. And I *will* write to them. And to you, of course. Do you think you're ever going to go back?'

'I'm not sure yet. Bill's here, and he's the most important thing in my life right now. I'm doing okay for work here. And I'm getting used to this crappy weather.' Actually, it's sunny today for the first time in months.

Daffodils are starting to appear in the shops and Easter cards and summer clothes. I suppose I will miss London a bit. This flat has really started to feel like home and it will be terrible without Caitlin. But this is the kind of thing I've always wanted to do. I can't give up the chance of happiness (or learning to surf). I told Lucy yesterday that I'll be leaving. She was more disappointed than I expected. We've just started to get closer and I know she's already short-staffed. I think Wendy's going to try and find a couple of third-year students who can work on The Laughing Duck and get credit towards their degree for it. Maybe she can come out for a visit. We can do the whole Byron Bay thing. She'd like that.

Bruce and I sit squashed up together on the sofa. We watch the late night edition of *Jerry Springer*, which is hysterical – 'Sisters Who Sleep Together'. I promise Bruce that one day we'll go to Chicago and be in the studio audience.

I'm almost sorry when Tyrone and Bill get back. It's so comfortable spending time with Bruce. He's like a second brother to me. Tyrone's wearing the shirt I gave him. It looks good, brings out the blue in his eyes. I feel more grown-up suddenly. I suppose making big decisions always does that to you. Makes you feel more responsible somehow, even if the decisions aren't good ones. But this one definitely is. It's going to be like living in *Home and Away*. And that can't be a bad thing.

*

Unbelievably, it's Declan and Jenny's wedding next weekend. The last few weeks have flown by. The four of us have clubbed together and bought them a gorgeous painting of a small church surrounded by green fields. It's actually of a place only about five miles from Declan's parents' house. Bill found it in a small gallery somewhere near his flat.

So it's Tyrone's last Saturday night in London and we're all going to The Blue Note. Caitlin and Paul are coming too. Caitlin and I get ready together. It's great. I borrow some of her glittery white eye shadow and she uses some of my Elizabeth Arden lip gloss. I'm wearing a black Chinese-style dress with a split that practically reaches my crotch. There's a white glittery rose motif on the back, hence the eye shadow. Caitlin's in a short white dress which is more Ibiza than Islington, but Paul's apparently a legs man.

We get tanked up on cheap sparkling wine and vodka and orange before we even leave the flat. I love the anticipation of a night out. It's sometimes better than the actual night out itself. Tyrone's wearing the shirt I gave him (again), and a pair of tight blue jeans finished off with a pair of Caterpillar boots. Maybe everyone dresses like that in Australia. That's a worrying thought. Nobody will even realise that I'm at the cutting edge of fashion. I'll have to get Caitlin to send me the British edition of Vogue every month.

We get to the club around midnight. Paul's waiting nervously outside. I'm sure this is not the kind of place he brings his wife to. There are four floors in the Blue Note and we soon split up and lose each other. Caitlin and I spend the first ten minutes in the loos touching up our make-up. Paul seems okay being left with the guys. He *is* a bit stiff though. He needs to get some more drink down him. Cheesy, happy music is playing on the top floor and Caitlin and I go in. Tyrone and Bruce are already at the bar and we shout our orders to them. What a relief not to have to join that queue. We manage to find seats but they *are* in a particularly chilly spot, right under the air-conditioning vent. We'll have to get up on the dance floor and warm up a bit. An ancient Jacksons track comes on and we jump to our feet.

I'm having one of those nights that you never want to end. The people are all amazingly friendly here and I'm totally relaxed and happy. We've been up and down checking out the different DJs but Caitlin and I keep coming back to the top floor. We've been dancing for what seems like hours and my feet still aren't hurting *too* much. Paul's loosened up a lot. He's great on the dance floor - lots of Travolta moves. Caitlin looks radiant, even though she's spilled vodka and cranberry down the front of her dress. We're all at that stage of being drunk but not too drunk. You know, merry but not at the point of feeling the whole room start to spin or desperately lurching towards the toilets. I'm trying to pace myself. It was £10 to get in and I can't actually afford to drink much more than I already have.

I sit down for a break with Bruce and Bill and we do that whole fashion police thing. 'God, look at that girl's bustier. She's going to fall out the top of it any second. And that guy's trousers... What *was* he thinking when he put those on?' Bruce and Bill are great at this and I start to get worried that we're being really obvious. I don't want to actually offend anybody. As long as they're happy, that's the main thing. (But that sweater with the sheep on is *totally* unacceptable.)

It can't be long before the club closes and I decide it's time to get smoochy with Tyrone. He's not dancing with Paul and Caitlin any more so I have to launch a search mission. It's so busy now and it's a real squeeze getting up and down the stairs. My wedge sandals make it even trickier. Somebody spills beer down the back of my dress but I'm past the point of caring. I just want to find Tyrone.

The ground floor isn't as packed as the rest of the place and that's where I finally find him. Only he isn't alone. He's pressed up against a girl in a black pencil skirt with a tight black cardigan and blonde hair. I know I shouldn't be noticing these things, but she has the most amazing shoes on. Furry black ones, like Eskimo shoes. I don't know what to do. He hasn't seen me. Since he's mid-snog and his eyes are closed it's not really surprising. I can't believe this is happening. I have to find Caitlin. I spend the next twenty minutes frantically pushing my way back up to where I left her. She's not there. It's another ten minutes before I find her getting a bottle of water at the bar.

I didn't know how upset I was until I start talking. My voice is verging on the hysterical and I know I'm not making much sense. The music is so loud. When I finally manage to explain what's happened it's obvious that Caitlin doesn't know what to do or say. She just keeps repeating 'Shit, Kell. Are you totally *sure* it was him?' Of course I'm fucking sure. I desperately want to leave *now*, and I tell Caitlin that I'm going outside to get a taxi. She won't let me go on my own and tells me to stay exactly where I am while she goes to tell Paul that she's taking me home. I remember to give her my cloakroom ticket to give to Bruce. I definitely can't be bothered hanging around for half an hour to get my coat back. It's not exactly my first priority right now. Caitlin says she'll give him her ticket as well.

It's freezing cold outside and we get into the first available cab. It's a dodgy minicab again. Why do I keep saying I'm never going to use one of these and then always do? I alternate between furious and pathetic all the way home. The stupid, ugly, insensitive piece of shit. Oh my God, I *love* him. What am I gonna do?

The first thing at least is simple. I throw all his stuff out of my room. Most of it lands haphazardly across the hall, although his black jeans make it as far as the lounge. I want to write a note to leave for him to read when he gets home, telling him not to bother coming into my bed tonight, but Caitlin says that probably won't be necessary. 'Okay Kell, he may be a thick, ungrateful wanker but he's not going to require a note when he sees last week's boxer shorts hanging from a picture frame on the wall in the hallway.'

Caitlin is a star. She tells me that it probably looked worse than it actually was. Some floozy probably just threw herself at him and he *was* pretty far gone. If I'd hung around longer she says I would have seen him push the girl away and tell her that he's got a girlfriend. I know Caitlin's my best friend and I know she's only saying these things to make me feel better but I can't help wanting to believe it all. Maybe there's still hope. I was going to buy suitcases on Monday. Surely one careless kiss can't wreck my whole life? I suppose it depends on what Tyrone's explanation is. If he even comes back, that is. Maybe he'll just shack up with the bleached-blonde bimbo and phone Bruce to tell him to send his stuff round.

I've smoked fifteen cigarettes before I put sheets on the fold-down bed for Caitlin. I smoke another two before I lie down myself. Of course, it's impossible to sleep. I'm so hyper from nicotine and so stressed out by Tyrone. I put on a Tori Amos CD with the volume low and it helps me relax a bit. Half of me doesn't want tomorrow to come but the other half is dying to get it over with and to know that everything's going to be okay. The white beach towel is draped over my chair, the price tag still on it.

CHAPTER TWENTY-EIGHT

The first thing I see when I wake up is a huge jug of daffodils on my desk. Caitlin is still asleep. It looks like Tyrone picked the flowers from somebody's garden on his way home last night. It's not even like he *bought* them. Not that I'm saying that I don't like them though. Bruce must have told him that I'd witnessed his little indiscretion. I decide to go back to sleep for a couple of hours, reluctant to face Tyrone. I hate confrontations.

*

When I finally get up at around midday Tyrone is still sleeping. The cheek! I'm not going to make the first move so I make a big fry-up instead. I'm sure cholesterol raises happiness levels. Caitlin comes through and we stuff our faces. I think Bruce has gone out for a cycle. I hope he brings back the paper. Just when we've finished breakfast we hear the toilet flush. Caitlin says she'll leave me to it. I thank her profusely for being there for me last night. It occurs to me suddenly that there's some poor woman at home completely unaware of the fact that her husband is sleeping with my best friend. It's a weird thought because the way I feel today, I can totally sympathise with Paul's wife. But Caitlin and I go back a long way and I guess our loyalties always lie with those who have been with us through thick and thin (unfortunately, in my case, more 'thick' than 'thin' if we're talking dress sizes).

Tyrone comes through to the kitchen. He's wearing a pair of red boxer shorts and a yellow Tower of London T-shirt. I feel myself weakening and I fight the urge to laugh at him. I pretend to be fascinated by the back of a cereal box. A special offer on a trip to a health farm if you collect forty-six of the special coupons. I wonder how many bowls of cereal that is.

'Kell, don't be mad. I was stupid. It's because I was drunk. It won't happen again. Want to come back to bed?' Every nerve in my body says 'yes', but I can't be such a pushover. I have to make him suffer a bit.

'I think that trust is the most important thing in a relationship, Tyrone.' (Well, apart from great sex, that is.) 'You really hurt me last night. I had plenty of opportunities to get off with sexy blokes at that club but I didn't just forget about *you* and go for it in a dark corner.' (There *was* the one guy who offered to buy me a drink. I would have said yes if he hadn't had such a bad stutter and looked like he was about forty.) 'A bunch of nicked daffodils isn't going to cut it. How do I know that you won't do the same thing again when the opportunity next presents itself?'

'Shit, it was just a kiss, Kelly. Chill out and get off my back. I didn't expect you to be *this* uptight about it.'

And I didn't expect him to give up the grovelling quite so fast. The nerve of the man. I want to get up and leave the flat, slamming the door behind me in a grand gesture. But I'm only wearing my bloody pyjamas so I have to make do with going for a shower. I slam the bathroom door. The effect is not nearly as good.

It must be about five minutes later when I hear a knock on the door. My eyes are full of shampoo and I grab a towel and rub them dry. 'What do you want?' God. Men are such a hassle. 'Are you on the dunny or in the shower? I want to scrub your back. Come on, Kell, don't leave me out here in the hall. I'm cold.' I think about what he said and decide to begin negotiations. 'If you promise to give me a back massage with baby oil, I might just consider opening the door. Oh, and you buy dinner tonight.' It's silent out there. Maybe I pushed him too hard. 'Hey, Kell. I'm back. I forgot my towel. You gonna let me in?'

I give in and open the door, modestly holding a towel in front of me. I don't offer much resistance when Tyrone pulls it off and stands there staring. 'You've got shampoo in your belly button.' I tell him to lick it out and the next hour turns into one of the best I've ever lived through. I think this actually makes up for the distress he caused last night, not that I'd ever tell him that though.

*

I make the dreaded phone call to my parents in the afternoon, while Tyrone picks up his clothes from the floor. It doesn't go as well as I'd hoped. My mother immediately asks if I've got a 'proper' job yet. I tell her as calmly as I can manage that I'm not looking for a job in London any more. That I think the prospects might be better in Perth. 'Well, your aunt Sheila and uncle Bob live just outside of Perth. Maybe they could put you up in their spare bedroom.'

'Perth, Australia, mother. Not *Scotland*. They're crying out for people with degrees there. In fact, I've already contacted a few people and it looks like I might have a job by the time I arrive.' My mother is actually speechless for a few moments but then she clicks into battle mode. She goes on and on about how I can't keep moving around nomadically, never settling in one place, never starting to build up a good pension. When I threaten to hang up she says, 'But we only want to see you *happy*, darling. That's all we've ever wanted.'

Bollocks. All they've ever wanted is for me to make *them* happy. I can't stand much more of this. I think optimistically about the extortionate price of phone calls to Australia. 'Well, I'm going whatever you say. And I *will* be happy. I'm going with Tyrone. He's my boyfriend. We're together. He gives me flowers every week and he's got a great house out there and he's going to help me out until I get settled.' What a vivid imagination I have at times.

*

I phone Sarah in the afternoon and arrange to meet her in a bar in Covent Garden. 'No, Tyrone *won't* be there.' I don't want to leave for Australia with things the way they are between us. And I also want to gloat about my upcoming new life Down Under.

She's already there by the time I arrive. When I've brought her up to date on my plans she's almost green with envy. But we do clear the air. She tells me that she honestly didn't know that Tyrone and I were sleeping together and says she wouldn't have come on so strong last week if she had. Yeah, well I'm not so sure about that, but it doesn't matter any more. Soon there'll be a couple of continents between them.

We spend a few hours drinking coffee after coffee and gossiping about anyone and everyone. I almost choke when Sarah tells me that she's applied to go on *Blind Date*. The audition's next week. I can't stop laughing and we start coming out with ridiculous questions she should ask if she gets on. 'If you were an item of women's lingerie, what would you be, and why? Where would you most like to be caught having sex – your parents' bed, in your office, or in the frozen goods section of Safeway's?' We can't stop giggling and people are starting to look at us strangely. I'm glad I made the effort to see Sarah. We do have a good laugh whenever we're together. I tell her that she has to video her *Blind Date* appearance and send it to me in Australia.

*

Tyrone does take me out for dinner after all. And it was *his* idea. We go to an Italian not far from the flat. Neither of us can be bothered getting the tube anywhere. I order cannelloni and Tyrone has pizza. I try not to appear too disgusted when he licks some tomato sauce off his knife. I'm sure it's just an Australian thing. I start talking about Sarah and I open up and tell him how much I hated it when she was so obviously interested in him. He says that he hadn't actually noticed that, and that he doesn't fancy her anyway because she's too skinny. At first I'm overjoyed to hear that he was never even interested in her, but then I think a bit more about what he said and get seriously paranoid again. Sarah's only one dress size smaller than me. Do I really look that huge? I don't finish the cannelloni, even though it's excellent.

As we walk back Tyrone tells me about his home town. It's on the outskirts of Perth and is mainly inhabited by commuters. Sounds like Slough to me. But hotter. He says that since he lost the job at the construction site he usually spends his days helping his mate Kenny do up cars that he buys for next to nothing. That he's hoping to save up some money and buy a 'ute' of his own. I don't think I like the sound of that. It's okay though. He explains that it's just a pick-up truck thing. 'But you *are* going to look into getting a new job when you go back, aren't you?' It's not like I want to *change* him or anything. But how can we do the kitchen in stainless steel if he's not bringing home any money? He says that he'll definitely get around to it when he's caught up with all his friends. He tells me that he wants to take back some Boddington's beer for them but that he's worried it won't fit into his rucksack. I think I'm going to be a good influence on Tyrone. His mother will probably adore me. I've never found the idea of having a house-husband appealing and if I get a job he'd bloody well better find one too. He stops at least three times on the way back to inspect motorbikes at close range. I hop around impatiently from one foot to the other. I'm not wearing my big coat and I'm cold. And my shoes are rubbing. I'll have to find a couple of Band-Aids when I get in.

Next door's cat is sitting on the doorstep when we get back to the flat. I go and make a big fuss over him, picking him up and cuddling him. Tyrone looks completely unimpressed. 'Never liked cats myself. Always wanted a pitbull though. They're introducing all these new laws in Australia these days and it's getting bloody expensive to get one. Put that thing down, let's get inside and see what's on the telly.' I reluctantly put the cat down. I'm surprised at Tyrone's words. I always expect everyone to like cats as much as I do and I really wish Tyrone did. I'd planned on getting a kitten as soon as we moved in together. Maybe this is something we should discuss further. In fact, there's probably quite a lot I should ask him about. Like, what's in his music collection? What do his parents do? Does he like ice-cream? Still, I suppose these are all minor worries. We do get on fantastically well and I think he'll take good care of me. I hope that I can meet some girls of my own age to hang about with. I'll leave the beer and brake fluid to Tyrone.

Bruce has just started watching a video of *Braveheart*. We join him and I get coffee for the three of us. I marvel at Mel Gibson's legs while Tyrone marvels at all the blood. Says there's more than you see in the low-budget Aussie-made horror movies he watches at home all the time. I prefer romantic comedies. I suddenly get a ridiculously strong patriotic feeling towards Scotland. All those green hills. And the kilts. I mention proudly that I visited the Bannockburn Visitor's Centre on a school trip in 1983. Or maybe it was 1984. Bruce and Tyrone don't seem to hear me.

I go to bed and leave the boys watching a football game that actually took place yesterday. What's the point? They already know the score. I have this weird uneasy feeling in my stomach. I guess it's just nerves about leaving the security of all my friends in London. Maybe if I get a good job I'll be able to come home at Christmas. Tyrone can come too, and meet my parents.

*

I have horrible dreams. Tyrone and my mother are having sex in the fridge in my house. My father is wearing a kilt and eating ice-cream while they do it. Bruce comes in and he's wearing high heels. He tells me that he's found me a job as a mechanic. The hours are six in the morning until six at night, six days a week. I wake up in a cold sweat. Tyrone's beside me and he's snoring so loudly that I can't get back to sleep for hours.

CHAPTER TWENTY-NINE

Yesterday was my last day on The Laughing Duck. I'm still not sure when I'll be following Tyrone out to Australia but I've been looking into flights for a fortnight after he goes. I'll have heaps to do anyway, and Lucy's managed to get two students to help out until she finds someone permanent. It was awful saying goodbye to the kids. Most of them didn't understand that I won't be back next week but *I* knew. I gave David the biggest hug. He told me to stop because he was going to break. He told me that his Ghostbusters man broke because he hugged him too hard. I brought Smarties for everyone and they'll probably always remember me for that, if nothing else.

It's three o'clock on Saturday afternoon and we're in imminent danger of being late for the wedding. There's a football game that the boys forgot about and the roads are horribly busy. Bill's borrowed his brother Peter's BMW so we're travelling to Surrey in style. Bill and Bruce are in the front and I'm squashed against Tyrone in the back. The car's very spacious actually, I just choose to be squashed against Tyrone. He's looking so much smarter than I've ever seen him look before. He's borrowed a pair of black trousers from Bruce and he found a stunning deep red shirt in the bottom of his rucksack. It took me about an hour to iron it for him. I've always had a problem with ironing. The only training

I've had is getting my Brownies Home Skills badge when I was nine. We all had to iron a tea towel. No wonder I find shirts so difficult. I'm wearing an indigo-coloured strapless dress with matching shoes. I'm almost as tall as Tyrone with these on. The boys have got bright yellow carnations in their buttonholes and I've got one in my hair.

Madonna's on the stereo and the sun looks like it's trying to come out. I remembered to bring my camera and I want to take loads of pictures. Lucy's going to be there. We offered her a lift but she says that she's going to take a good book and get the train. Says she hasn't seen fields from a train window since she was tiny. I suppose it will make a nice change from the tube. Tyrone keeps touching my hair and I have to keep pushing his hand away. The style I've done is very precarious. Bill and Bruce are arguing over the map. I'm pretty sure neither of them know how to read it or where we are, but Jenny said there are lots of signs so it shouldn't be that difficult. Tyrone wants to put a Nirvana tape on but he's outvoted. I can't stop smiling, and I'm not even *at* the wedding yet.

We finally navigate our way to the registry office. We only had to stop and ask four people along the way. I hand out confetti to everyone in sight. There was a note on the invite saying that the local council would be grateful if well-wishers would refrain from throwing confetti as it poses a serious problem for the cleaning department. Fuck that. This is a wedding!

We've only been waiting for about five minutes when Declan and Jenny appear. They look so happy I have to grab for a Kleenex from my bag. I take about fifteen photos in the space of three minutes. It's raining confetti. There's no chance to talk to them though, they're absolutely mobbed. It's a very good sign when there are so many people eager to wish you well. Jenny's wearing the most beautiful lilac dress. It skims over her huge bump pretty well. It reminds me of the things they wore in the latest BBC production of *Pride and Prejudice*. We get back on the road after the wedding car's pulled away, and head for the country inn where the official photographs and meal are taking place. It's only a ten-minute drive, and this time there are people to follow. The countryside is beautiful. All the leaves are just appearing on the trees. I'm a bit disappointed that I don't see any lambs frolicking in the fields though.

Lucy's already there by the time we arrive. She's wearing a flowery Laura Ashley dress which really suits her. The place itself is charming. It's a Tudor style building and there are flowers growing all over the place. I take a couple of photos of some of the best ones. Unfortunately it's a non-smoking dining room so a large group of smokers congregates outside before going in to eat. When we do go in I find to my horror that I'm not sitting beside Tyrone. He's at a totally different table. I've got a banker on my left called Mark and a farmer on my right called Giles. I strain my neck to see where Tyrone's been placed. There's a horsy looking girl on one side of him. She looks about fifteen. On his other side is one of the numerous elderly aunts of the bride. Thank God. At least I can relax and enjoy the meal. And it is an absolutely perfect meal. The starter is smoked salmon with a dill sauce. Then half the room, including Declan's father, nip outside for a cigarette. The main course is a choice of veal or chicken. I go for the chicken which is gorgeous. I've always hated the idea of people eating veal. I really would be a vegetarian if I didn't like McDonalds so much. Another cigarette follows. The dessert is bramble mousse and I make a note to ask somebody for the recipe. It's amazing. Kind of like sorbet except much creamier and not so cold. I shouldn't really have eaten so much. Now I'm going to have to concentrate on holding my tummy in for the rest of the evening. I can't even move to go and have another cigarette.

There are speeches over the cheese board and coffee. Most of them are a bit boring. Maybe it's just because I'm feeling sleepy after that huge meal. Declan's speech is the biggest surprise. It totally wakes me up. I don't even know if the groom usually does a speech. Anyway, he talks about how happy and excited he and Jenny are to be starting a family. He makes some corny joke about how they had to move the date of the wedding forward just because Jenny was so stubborn about the dress she wanted. Everyone laughs politely. Then he drops the bombshell. The reason Jenny's stomach has been growing so enormous is that she's actually expecting twins! The whole room breaks out into a spontaneous round of applause. Seems they only found out a few days ago when Jenny had a scan. I think I'd find two kittens a handful, let alone two screaming babies. But if they take after their parents they'll probably be very happy, contented kids.

More drinking and dancing follows. We all get our chance to take photographs and congratulate the happy couple. Declan and Jenny absolutely adore the painting we gave them. Lucy takes a photo of me and Declan. I hold in my stomach and hope that my face isn't shiny or my hair drooping. Then Tyrone takes one of me and Lucy. I feel like this wedding has given me the best chance ever to spend time with my closest friends before I start a whole new life abroad.

We leave at about eleven. Bill has to get the car back to his brother and Tyrone's got to be at the airport early. The wedding's been the perfect distraction for me. I was looking forward to it so much and now it's all over. Tyrone won't be here this time tomorrow and I haven't even got my plane ticket yet. I know the phone bill over the next few days is going to be terrifying. I'll have to get Bruce to send it to me in Australia.

*

I don't want to go to sleep. I feel like Tyrone and I should make full use of every minute we still have together. But we *have* been doing that for at least two hours and quite frankly, we're both absolutely knackered. Tyrone's stuff is all ready and it's sitting beside the front door. He only managed to fit in twelve cans of beer in the end. I've pushed a little card into the front pocket of his rucksack. He'll find it when he's home. It just tells him how much I've enjoyed the last month we've spent together and that he has to hurry up and find a place for us. I couldn't come up with any words that really conveyed how important he is to me. Even if he *is* a bastard at times.

I'm not going to the airport. It'd just be too horrible. I'd probably get myself into such a state that I wouldn't be able to find my way back home. Bruce offered to go with him, but Tyrone said he'll be okay taking the Heathrow Express. I can't bear to think about it. My bed's going to feel so big without him.

*

The morning is quickly upon us and it's a mad panic. Somehow the alarm didn't go off until half an hour after it was meant to. Tyrone and I don't even have time for a quickie, and I feel horribly cheated. I wouldn't be too upset if he *missed* the bloody plane. I ask him a zillion times if he's sure he's remembered everything. He starts to get annoyed and tells me I sound like his mother. I start crying and he hugs me hard and tells me that he's just crabby because I didn't let him get enough sleep last night. Then he smiles his sexy smile and says that he's not complaining. God, we're going to have a lot of catching up to do when I arrive in Oz.

Bruce is standing around with sleepy eyes. I know he's going to miss Tyrone too. He's been a little piece of home for Bruce. When the time approaches for him to leave they do a lot of slapping each other on the back stuff, and Bruce says he's going to do his best to go home for a holiday later in the year. Tyrone says he'll have the barbie and the stubbies (stubbies?) ready. I feel like everything's slipping out of my control. No bolt of lightening has stopped Tyrone in his tracks and the last couple of minutes are really upon us.

He puts down his bag and throws his arms around me. He lifts me up and spins me around. 'Thanks for being such a good tour guide, babe. Hope I can return the favour in the not too distant future.' I'm too choked up to reply. I just kiss him like my life depends on it. And in a way it does.

*

The next week or so is horrific. The weather has gone back to winter and the grey days match my mood. Tyrone still hasn't phoned or written. It takes about a week for a letter to get from Australia to here so it could be any day now. Everything seems so quiet. No Tyrone, no Laughing Duck, no laughing full stop. Bruce has been very understanding but I know he thinks I'm acting a bit over the top considering I'll be seeing Tyrone again in a couple of weeks. Feels more like a couple of months. Why hasn't he written? I've phoned the number he gave me four times. The first three times there was no answer and the fourth time I spoke to his mother. She didn't even seem to recognise my name. Maybe Tyrone's still working out the best way to tell her about us. Anyway, she told me she'd tell him I'd rung, but that was two days ago and still no word. Nights are the worst. I've gotten so used to feeling the bulk of Tyrone lying beside me. It was comforting somehow, even when he was asleep. Just knowing someone's beside you, keeping you warm, skin against skin. (Although I did have to resort to pyjamas on the particularly cold nights.)

*

The airmail letter comes for me on Tuesday. My whole life is about to change. I don't know whether to be happy or petrified. I think a bit of both is healthy. It's time I start making something out of my life. Time I make my mark. Oh God. Before I know it, it's time to say goodbye to Bruce and Caitlin. I hate goodbyes.

CHAPTER THIRTY

Things to Pack

4 sundresses
3 pairs of shorts
1 pair of jeans
6 tops
little black dress
knickers
bras
3 pairs of <u>low-heeled</u> shoes
suntan oil
towels
make-up
hairdryer
camera
money and travellers' cheques
passport
photo of Fluffy

*

I'm going to the airport on my own. I'd probably chicken out if anyone came with me. I'm pretty sure I'm doing the right thing. But this is not easy. Not at all. My mother was on the phone last night for at least half an hour. 'Have they got telephones there, darling? Will you phone and tell us as soon as you arrive?' Deep down I like her worrying. I know it's just her way of showing how much she cares. I didn't forget to use the Harrods voucher she gave me before I left London. I had all the knots of tension pummelled out of my body on Friday, by a large Bulgarian man called Boris.

I nipped across to Covent Garden yesterday and bought the most amazing stainless steel vanity case. And loads of those refillable toiletries bottles from Muji. My sunglasses are on my head, holding back my hair and I'm wearing a camel-coloured two-piece suit. I think it could be mistaken for a Chanel, from a distance. I experience this surge of independence as I walk through the entrance to Departures. I hope I look like a film star, or failing that, at least a TV presenter. That's the image I'm aiming for.

Check-in goes smoothly. I'm not embarrassed by my passport photo for once. Last time I renewed my passport I went to the Photo-Me booth twelve times until I got a picture I was really happy with. I *had* hoped to travel light but it didn't work out that way. I just wasn't strong enough to limit myself to only taking the stuff on my Things to Pack list. My two cases disappear along the conveyor belt. Sixteen kilos each. There's no going back now.

The duty-free shop is the usual paradise of discount make-up, perfume and fags. I don't have room in my hand luggage for much more, but I manage to find enough space for some Clinique Seven Day Scrub and two hundred *Cosmopolitan* cigarettes. They're American and they look very sophisticated. The filter's white. I have to keep an eye on my watch or I'll risk getting so distracted by the new Yves Saint Laurent perfume that I'll miss the call for my flight.

I head through to the departure lounge. It's fascinating watching people at airports. Where's he going? In that shirt, my guess is Hawaii.

And that old couple. This must be really intimidating for them. At least they're sitting close to one of the airline ground staff. I'm sure that a couple of businessmen stop and do a double take when they walk past me. God, I'm glad I wore this suit.

I make myself comfortable in the smoking area and take out the latest copy of Vogue that I bought in the airport bookshop. I can't travel anywhere without a lot of reading material. I've also got a new book of crosswords from Bruce. I'm really going to miss him.

I haven't even finished my cigarette when I hear the call over the Tannoy. '*Flight BA946 to Tel Aviv is now ready for boarding. Would all passengers please make their way to gate two*.'

The job is only a junior position, I know, but I don't mind starting at the very bottom and working my way up. In fact, I'm positively looking forward to embarking on my new career. I've got a twelve-month contract to start off with, but it'll be extended if they're happy with me. I've finally got a chance to prove myself. The broadcasting company are sending a car to meet me at Tel Aviv airport and they've arranged an apartment for me. That's more than can be said of Tyrone. He's probably drinking beer and working on some front axle at this very moment. I was desperate for *something*, and I made myself believe that Tyrone was it. I know it was all a dream though. I was looking for an escape from the rut I felt I was stuck in and Tyrone came along at the right moment (or the wrong moment, depending on how you look at it). He did finally phone, but by that time I'd already received the job offer and thought about what I should really be doing with my life. The weather's good in Israel too. Tyrone didn't sound that put out. He could have at least *pretended*. He told me to keep his address and get in touch if I'm ever passing through his neighbourhood. I shouldn't really blame him. He came to London for a holiday and was probably more in need of one when he left. I guess I heaped a lot of expectations on the guy before I even got to know him. But no regrets. I can still see a faint bite mark on my left shoulder if I look at it in a certain light. We certainly made some good memories.

Fluffy is staying with Bruce. I don't want to disrupt him and it's better if he has some continuity in his life. I think it would be too hot out there for him anyway. Bruce has promised to let him out to run around at least once a week. I know that he'll be in good hands but I wish he was here with me.

Bill is planning to move into the flat with Bruce. Declan and Jenny's wedding might not have given Tyrone any ideas, but it definitely had a strong effect on those two. There's word of them tying the knot in a special ceremony later in the year. Their first choice of location is a ruined castle in Scotland. I wouldn't miss that for the world. Weddings are the only time I ever cry out of happiness. They've all promised that they're going to send me loads of photos of Declan and Jenny's twins when they're born.

Caitlin is still seeing Paul. It's bound to end in tears for one of them. I'm hoping it will be Paul. Maybe Caitlin will be swept off her feet by the owner of a French chateau. And he'll be rich, gorgeous and *single*. No matter what happens, or where I am in the world, Caitlin knows that I'll always be on the end of the phone. I'll probably be phoning her regularly. I've got her office number, home number and mobile number in my handbag, just in case.

Lucy has met a guy called Dillon and says that she might have only known him for a few days but she's pretty sure she's falling for him in a big way. He runs an organic fruit and veg company not far from where she lives. He loves hearing about The Laughing Duck and has told her that he'll come to lend a hand if she ever needs it. She did plant a tree in memory of Doris. It's on the bank of the canal and even if nobody else knows what it's there for, Frank knows. He's taken to visiting Lucy on the boat, bringing scones he buys in Safeway's.

Sarah passed the audition for *Blind Date* with flying colours. She wore the most outrageous white cat suit on the day and they can't wait to have her back. She can get away with that kind of thing with her tiny bum. She's promised she'll video it for me. Maybe she'll be picked and end up coming on a paragliding holiday in Israel.

My mother is planning to come out for a week's holiday in June with her friend Elizabeth. She's already bought two incredibly gaudy-sounding sarongs in honour of the occasion. I think it will be good for us to spend some time together on neutral ground. I'm going to send her brochures from hotels near where I'll be living just as soon as I find out where that is. We'll eat in restaurants every night and there'll be no pressure. (And probably hundreds of incredibly good-looking waiters.) My mother and I have a long way to go in achieving any kind of harmony but I think we're going to get there. A mother's love is a strange and wonderful thing.

*

The flight takes just over five hours. My first impressions of Israel are that it's as hot as I could ever want and that it's very dusty. The ground is like an assault course. I am *so* glad I brought these shoes. Although I couldn't resist slipping in one pair of extremely high black strappy sandals at the last minute. You know, always be prepared. I suppose I'll have to save them until I've got a man to hang onto.

The airport is comparatively small and it doesn't take long to clear customs. The few people I've talked to so far seem very friendly. This is such an adventure. I must buy some postcards as soon as I get the chance. I'd like to find one showing a beautiful beach or a stunning sunset, and send it to Cordelia. That'll show *her*. I think I'll send one to Mick and Kathryn too. It'll brighten up the switchboard room. I'm trying to take in everything around me to report back to Caitlin. If this job works out well I might be reporting on issues a lot more serious than that. It's such a challenge. I *so* want to be the next Kate Adie. I can just hear it: 'This is Kelly Stewart, reporting from Tel Aviv, Israel'. I realise that I've got quite a lot to learn in the meantime. Hebrew would be a good place to start.

I panic for a moment when I can't see anyone who looks like they're here to meet me. But then I notice a man holding a big white card with my name on it. He's standing beside a huge palm tree just outside the main entrance. I don't think I've ever felt so important. I go over to introduce myself. The closer I get, the more I think I'm going to like it here. The man holding the card must be in his early to mid thirties. He's got a deep tan, sparkling hazel eyes and great hair. Oh, and the sexiest accent *ever*. He immediately takes my trolley and is utterly charming and courteous. He guides me into a white Mercedes, one hand lightly on my shoulder. He speaks perfect English. He offers to show me around the city and to tell me about some of the local history and customs. I'm not going to jump into anything too quickly. I'm still learning from my mistakes. But there's no harm in taking things *slowly*. This could get interesting. I have to find a phone. Caitlin should still be at her desk.